THE PARKER FAMILY SECRET

KAY CORRELL

ZURA LU PUBLISHING, LLC

Published by Zura Lu Publishing LLC

This book is dedicated to my readers, my wonderful readers. You bring such joy to my life with your enthusiasm for my stories. You've made my career so meaningful and I thank each of you.

THE PARKER FAMILY SECRET

Donna and Evelyn's mother, Patricia, is… *difficult*, at best.

Patricia wants things her way, the proper way, of course. There can be no cause for gossip and she's not forgiven Heather for her big scandalous secret.

When Ted Cabot ends up in a condo right next to Patricia, she does everything possible to avoid him. Just because they were friends years ago does not mean that they need to be friends now.

And yet… they do slowly become friends again.

But those pesky Parker secrets have a way of popping up and turning everyone's world upside down. And this Parker Secret is a doozy.

MOONBEAM BAY - the series

Find more information on all my books at
kaycorrell.com

COMFORT CROSSING ~ THE SERIES

The Shop on Main - Book One
The Memory Box - Book Two
The Christmas Cottage - A Holiday Novella
(Book 2.5)
The Letter - Book Three
The Christmas Scarf - A Holiday Novella
(Book 3.5)
The Magnolia Cafe - Book Four
The Unexpected Wedding - Book Five

The Wedding in the Grove - (a crossover short

story between series - with Josephine and Paul from The Letter.)

LIGHTHOUSE POINT ~ THE SERIES
Wish Upon a Shell - Book One
Wedding on the Beach - Book Two
Love at the Lighthouse - Book Three
Cottage near the Point - Book Four
Return to the Island - Book Five
Bungalow by the Bay - Book Six

CHARMING INN ~ Return to Lighthouse Point
One Simple Wish - Book One
Two of a Kind - Book Two
Three Little Things - Book Three
Four Short Weeks - Book Four
Five Years or So - Book Five
Six Hours Away - Book Six
Charming Christmas - Book Seven

SWEET RIVER ~ THE SERIES
A Dream to Believe in - Book One
A Memory to Cherish - Book Two
A Song to Remember - Book Three
A Time to Forgive - Book Four
A Summer of Secrets - Book Five

A Moment in the Moonlight - Book Six

MOONBEAM BAY ~ THE SERIES
The Parker Women - Book One
The Parker Cafe - Book Two
A Heather Parker Original - Book Three
The Parker Family Secret - Book Four
Grace Parker's Peach Pie - Book Five
The Perks of Being a Parker - Book Six

INDIGO BAY ~ A multi-author sweet romance series

Sweet Days by the Bay - Kay's Complete Collection of stories in the Indigo Bay series

Or buy them separately:

Sweet Sunrise - Book Three
Sweet Holiday Memories - A short holiday story
Sweet Starlight - Book Nine

Sign up for my newsletter at my website *kaycorrell.com* to make sure you don't miss any new releases or sales.

CHAPTER 1

Patricia Beale stood in her penthouse condo at the Sunrise Village Retirement Community. She frowned in annoyance. The movers had put a scratch in her favorite mahogany table. A small one that they assured her they could fix, but it still irritated her. She ran her finger along the blemish. Could no one do their job anymore?

Not to mention, the whole move had been a disaster. First, the movers had gotten the date mixed up… she was sure it wasn't *her* mistake. So, her move had been delayed by a week. And now she wasn't happy at all with the main room after telling them where to place the furniture.

To pique her further, the large windows

overlooking the bay had wooden blinds on them… which she wasn't fond of. She'd have to get some custom drapes made.

She sighed. She should probably call the interior designer she'd used before when she lived in Moonbeam Bay. Now what was her name? Maybe she'd redo everything in the condo. New furniture. New window treatments. An unsettled feeling wrapped around her and she detested it. She was used to her life falling neatly into place, just like she wanted it to.

Well, except for Donna getting married at such an inconvenient time a few weeks ago. Why her daughter had decided to get married at her age was a puzzlement. But then her girls never did listen to her like they should.

She sank onto the couch and looked around the room, suddenly tired. Boxes piled into towers in all the corners of the room. How in the world was she supposed to unpack all of that and get things sorted out? She didn't remember it being this difficult the last time she moved.

And it annoyed her that her friends who had also moved here from their last retirement place in Naples were already unpacked and settled in, while her place was in disarray. She would talk to the concierge and see if she could hire someone to come unpack all of this. She was certain—positive—that she'd hired the movers to do the unpacking, too. Obviously, they'd messed up that part of their agreement, too.

Light streamed in through the windows and filtered across the tile floor. The floor that needed cleaning after all the movers had traipsed across it. She'd have to ask about a cleaning service, too. The village staff had assured her all units were thoroughly cleaned before anyone moved in, and since the community was brand new, no one had lived here before her. Still, the apartment felt dirty after all the people who'd been in here today.

She also needed to get some basic groceries delivered. Her favorite tea and some cereal if she didn't feel like going downstairs to the dining room to eat breakfast. She wasn't much for jumping in and seizing the day. She liked a slow start to her mornings.

But she really should consider going down to the dining room now. She wasn't sure if it was still open for lunch or not. If not, they did have a small area they called a cafe where you could order soup, salad, or a sandwich. Maybe she'd do that and bring it up here to her condo. Although, she had no idea where her dishes were or which box to unpack to find them. A long sigh escaped her lips.

Moving had been altogether a *very* unpleasant task.

Olivia looked up from where she was clearing the dishes off of a table at the Sea Glass Cafe and her face broke into a spontaneous smile. She set down the tray and rushed over to the entrance, throwing herself into Austin's waiting arms.

"You're back early," she finally managed to say after a long hug and several kisses.

"I am. I missed you, Livy. Caught an earlier flight." He looked down at her, his arms still wrapped around her. His eyes looked tired.

She held him tight before finally taking a step back. "I missed you too." She reached up and pushed her messy hair back away from her face. She'd planned to rush home from work, shower, and change before Austin got home. That plan mocked her now.

Her daughter, Emily, came rushing up to them. "Austin, you're back."

"Hey, Emily. You been keeping busy while I was gone?"

"Sure have. Here and at the historical museum. Oh, and I worked on the cafe's social media more. Did you see that? Mom is opening up a new seasonal room at the store. I'm doing promo for that. We're going to have a grand opening for it. Kind of like we did for the cafe, but not quite so big." Emily's details came rushing out at them.

Livy grinned at her daughter's enthusiasm, then looked at Austin. The man had a semi-dazed look on his face. She elbowed him. "Catch up, buddy. Lots happened while you were gone."

"It appears so."

"Mom, you should go. I'll finish up here. And you might want to run home and, uh, change."

She looked down at her outfit. A Parker's General Store t-shirt with a stain on it, she was just now noticing. She turned to Austin. "Could you give me a bit of time to wrap things up here and go change?"

"Absolutely. I'll pick up steaks to grill out tonight and head home. Meet me there?"

"That sounds great."

"Perfect, I'll see you there in a bit." He kissed her quickly on the cheek and headed back out the door.

"He's a good one, Mom. Don't screw this one up." Emily tossed the words and a grin as she turned and walked away.

Olivia had no plans whatsoever of screwing this relationship up. None at all.

Patricia found her purse and the silly ID she was supposed to have with her to purchase food at the village. Hopefully, the staff would get to know her and this ridiculous ID thing would end. She absolutely refused to clip it on her outfit or wear it on the lanyard they'd given her. Ridiculous. Just utterly ridiculous.

She searched around for the door key. Though it wasn't a key, really. It was one of those newfangled door cards that she'd have to use to get into her condo. State-of-the-art security, the village had assured her. Maybe, but she much preferred a good old-fashioned real key. On a good old-fashioned key ring.

She found the keycard by a stack of paperwork she'd been given upon move-in. A calendar of the week's activities along with hours for the meals. Glancing at the paper, she realized she had missed lunch in the dining room. So the cafe it was.

With one last look at the disarray that was her new home, she headed out the door, pulling it tightly behind her, listening for the click to make sure it was locked. She swiveled around and froze, her hand suspended in the air.

"Patricia." Ted Cabot stood a few steps down the hall from her, the last person she expected or wanted to see.

She tried to say his name, but nothing came out. She just stood frozen to the spot.

He crossed the distance to her, a warm smile on his face. "So, it looks like we're neighbors here at Sunrise Village. Now that's some coincidence, isn't it?"

"Ah…"

"I see you got a penthouse suite, too. Magnificent view, don't you think?"

She nodded. Still no words.

"I was just headed down to get something

from the cafe. I'm afraid I got so wrapped up in unpacking the last of my things that I missed lunch."

She still just stood there, her heart pounding, not knowing what to say after all these years.

Ted seemed unaware of her problems and continued talking. "So, have you just moved in?"

"I did." There, she'd finally found some words.

"Are you headed downstairs?"

"I am." But now she no longer wanted to go to the cafe. She'd rather starve. Not if Ted Cabot was going to be there. Much too awkward. New plan. "I need to talk to the concierge and see if he can get someone to help with the unpacking. The moving company got everything mixed up."

"I could help with that. I've become quite the expert at it." He gave her another warm smile and his green eyes sparkled. They still looked the same, just a few more wrinkles around them when he smiled, but it only made his smile seem that much more charming and friendly.

He actually looked quite a bit the same. Still looked to be in great shape. He used to jog every day. Certainly, he didn't still do that at their age?

His hair was streaked with gray, but it was still thick with a hint of wave to it.

Wait? Had she just stood there staring at him without answering his offer? "I… I couldn't ask you to do that."

"You didn't. I offered. We could chat and catch up while we unpack. It's been a long time."

She stared at him for a moment. What had he just suggested? No way. "Ah… thanks for the offer. It's kind. But I'll get someone to come in and do it."

"As you wish." He swept his arm out and held out a hand, motioning towards the elevator. Gallant and courteous as ever.

They walked down the hallway, side by side, and stood in front of the elevator, waiting.

How did this happen? How did she end up being the next-door neighbor to Ted Cabot?

She wasn't unpacked yet… she could see if she could get a different suite… But by now all the really nice ones were bound to be gone. Especially on the penthouse floor. She really did want to live on the penthouse floor. She could only hope she wouldn't keep running into him.

The door swept open, and she stepped inside. They rode down to the ground floor in silence, and Ted reached out to keep the door open as she exited. Still polite, still courteous. Some things never changed.

"Well, it was nice to see you, Patricia. I'm sure we'll see more of each other."

She gave him a weak smile and hoped he was wrong. Hoped he was very wrong. She'd like nothing more than to never see him again. Ever.

He turned and headed toward the cafe, his step still spry. Maybe he did still jog...

She headed to the lobby to figure out this unpacking mess. Betsy, one of her friends from the prior retirement community who had also moved here, waved to her as she entered the lobby.

Betsy. She didn't know why the woman insisted on being called Betsy instead of Elizabeth. Or even Beth. Betsy just seemed so casual and so young. They weren't young anymore.

Betsy hurried up to her. "Oh, you've finally arrived. We were beginning to worry about you."

"The movers messed things up. So much. And scratched my favorite table. And they didn't unpack. I must find help with that."

"Go talk to Eugene at the concierge desk.

He knows everyone and everything. I bet he can get it sorted out for you."

"I certainly hope so." And maybe if she lingered long enough, Ted would be gone from the snack area and she could get something to eat...

CHAPTER 2

Donna met her sister, Evelyn, in the parking lot of Sunrise Village late that afternoon. "You ready for this?" Donna asked looking up at the impressive, brand new building their mother had moved into.

Evelyn shrugged and gave her a wry grin. "As ready as I ever am to visit Mother. I wonder if the movers have left."

"I don't know. I don't see a van out here."

"Truth. Well, I hope she likes this place and gets settled in okay." Evelyn looked around. "It sure is lovely here. They did a great job with the grounds, didn't they?"

"And Mom has a room overlooking the bay, I heard. You know, from back when she was speaking to us." Donna rolled her eyes, which she was sure was the wrong thing to do regarding one's own mother. A flicker—a tiny one—flashed through her. Her relationship with her mother was… complicated.

"She's a bit upset about Blake. A shock to find out Heather had a son that no one knew about. But that's no reason to ignore us, or to hurt Blake's feelings. I've tried calling her, but she doesn't pick up." Evelyn sighed.

"I was actually surprised she showed up at my wedding. But then she just came over, said hi, and ran off. It was kind of strange…"

"It was. Then again, you never can predict how Mom is going to act."

Which was why they were going to try this surprise visit. She took her sister's arm in solidarity. "Come on, let's go up and see her. Hopefully she doesn't just slam the door in our faces."

They rode the elevator up to their mother's unit on the top floor. "Here it is," Donna said after passing by a few doors. "It's this one." She took a quick look at Evelyn, who nodded encouragingly.

She knocked on the door and waited. No

answer. She knocked again, louder. Still no answer.

"Maybe she's not here?" Evelyn said, then pointed at a small doorbell at the side of the door. "Let's try this." Evelyn jabbed the button.

"She must be here. She just moved in. Shouldn't she be here unpacking or something? I thought we could at least help with that. You know, if she ever answers the door and actually lets us in."

"Sh. I hear something." Evelyn stared at the door.

The door swung open, and their mother stood there with a not so welcoming look on her face. "Girls. I wasn't expecting you."

"Hi, Mom." Donna pasted on a wide smile. A friendly one. A *nice* one. "We thought we'd come see your new place. Did you get all moved in?"

"No. I did not. The movers messed up and didn't unpack. I specifically asked for a move that included unpacking. They said I didn't, but I know it's their mistake." Patricia's face contorted into her familiar look of disapproval and disdain.

"We could help," Evelyn offered.

Donna shot her an are-you-crazy look.

"I've already taken care of it with the concierge here at Sunrise. He's arranged for help tomorrow."

"Do you need anything unpacked for now?" Donna asked, trying to sound as helpful as Evelyn.

"I guess I'll go stay in a hotel this evening. With nothing unpacked and the bed not made, well… I can't stay here. Obviously." Patricia's face crinkled up in displeasure at the very idea.

"Mom, ask us in. We'll make up your bed and get some boxes opened with things you'll need tonight." Donna wasn't sure, but she thought her mother was wavering.

"It might be nice to stay here this evening. I'm not even sure where I have a suitcase to pack for an overnight stay at a hotel."

"Great, we'll help then." Evelyn breezed past their mother and into the condo.

Donna followed closely behind her sister, acutely aware their mother hadn't exactly asked them in.

"Mother, the place is beautiful." Evelyn stood in the middle of the room, turning slowly around in a circle.

"It is nice, Mom." Donna headed over to

the window. "Oh, wow. And look at your view." Moonbeam Bay sprawled out before her, sparkling in the sunlight.

Her mother ignored the remark about the view. "I'm thinking I'm going to have to replace the furniture. I'm not sure my furnishings are right for this place. Evelyn, I'm going to use that interior decorator that you use."

"Well, I don't use her anymore. Not at my apartment."

Patricia frowned. "Then how did you know how to decorate it?"

Evelyn laughed. "I've gone to the thrift store for most things. And Heather painted a few pieces for me. I think it looks really cute."

"It does. Just darling." Donna preemptively rushed to her sister's defense before their mother could say anything.

Patricia shook her head. "I've raised you better than shopping at a thrift store. You know that everything is *used* there, don't you?"

Donna grinned at Evelyn. "That's kind of the point? It's things people don't want anymore, but maybe someone else does. And the price is right."

"I don't understand you girls sometimes.

Used furniture? And then that whole distasteful mess with Heather."

"Mother—stop." Donna walked over to stand beside her sister. "It's not a mess. Heather had a son she gave up for adoption, but he's here now. Blake is a great kid."

"But people in town are talking, I'm sure."

"Maybe," Evelyn stood up to her mother. "But we don't care. He's great. Really, you should get to know him. He is your great-grandson, you know."

"I hope there's not going to be a lot of embarrassments like this now that I've moved back to Moonbeam." Patricia frowned. "It simply won't do. We have a family name to uphold."

"How about we start unpacking for you, Mom?" Donna changed the subject, knowing her mother was like a dog with a bone when she got on a tirade about something.

"I suppose I could let you do that."

What her mother meant to say was thank you very much, girls. It's so appreciated.

"We'll start in the bedroom and find your bedding." Donna grabbed her sister's hand and pulled her toward the bedroom.

"No, it's that way," Patricia pointed in the

opposite direction. "That side of the condo has the extra bedroom and den. Mine is over here."

They switched direction and went to their mother's bedroom. Donna eyed the stacks of boxes. "How are we ever going to find what we need?"

Evelyn went over to a stack and laughed. "The movers who packed her up were good. Look, each box is labeled with what's inside."

They sorted through boxes until they found the ones marked bedding and made up the bed for their mother. "Do you think Mom has ever made her own bed?" Evelyn whispered as she plunked down on the end of the bed when they finished.

"Probably not." Donna grinned.

"So, let's dig out some towels for her. And I saw a box that said bathroom. We'll move it into the bathroom and open it."

"I saw one that said toiletries. Let me find it again, and we'll haul that in for her, too."

At least the movers had moved the dresser with the drawers full, so their mother could find some clothing in there. And they must have moved the hanging clothes separately because all the clothes were hanging in the closet, Donna saw as she peeked in. Though, her mother would not be happy. She had a precise order of how she liked her clothes hung, and the movers had not taken notice of that. Dresses sorted by color. Slacks together, also by color, though you rarely saw her mother in slacks other than white or black. Then all the blouses hung by color. Nope, she wasn't much interested in sorting that out for her mother right now. She just wouldn't mention it.

They came out of the bedroom to find their mother sitting at a table in front of the window overlooking the bay. Leafing through a magazine, totally unconcerned about lifting a finger to help with the unpacking.

"You should be set for spending the night, now." Donna waited for a thank you.

Didn't happen.

"Could you girls find my teapot and cups? I'll want tea in the morning. I ordered groceries that were delivered a little bit ago." Patricia frowned. "I had to tip them extra to have them actually carry them to the kitchen. They wanted to leave them at the door. Can you imagine?"

"Hm," was all that Donna could manage to answer.

"Sure, Mom. We'll find them." Evelyn

headed to the kitchen and Donna trailed after her, rolling her eyes.

They found the teapot and cups and pulled out a few plates and bowls while they were at it. "Mom, we put the dishes we found in the cabinet to the right of the sink," Donna called out.

They came out to the main room where their mother was still leafing through the magazine. A fashion magazine, Donna noticed. Most of the people here at Sunrise Village seemed to be wearing a kind of dressy casual. Resort casual or some fancy name like that. They were all dressed nicer than Donna ever did on a daily basis. To each their own.

"Did you say that you put the dishes to the right of the sink?"

"Yep," Donna answered.

"Donna, don't say yep. That sounds so classless. The word is yes. And I think I might want the dishes on the other side."

"When the unpackers come tomorrow, why don't you go into the kitchen with them and sort things out however you'd like them," Evelyn suggested.

Their mother sighed. "I guess I'll have to if I want it done properly."

Donna wasn't certain that there was a proper way to have a kitchen, but who was she to contradict her mother? Her own kitchen still had all the dishes and pots and pans in the same cabinet her grandmother had them in. And probably her great-grandmother. Okay, she actually still had some of their *actual* pans...

"You sure you don't need help with anything else?" Evelyn, the much more charitable sister, offered. Because Donna was *so* ready to leave.

"No, that's fine. I'm going to meet a few friends down in the dining room soon. I hope the meals are as good here as they claimed."

"I'm sure they'll be great," Donna said with absolutely no knowledge if they would be or not, but certain her mother would find fault with them anyway.

"We'll go then," Evelyn said as she picked up her purse.

Their mother nodded but didn't get up. Nor thank them, for that matter, not that Donna really expected a thank you. Their mother was used to having people do things for her. Expected it.

"Bye, mother." She hurried after Evelyn and they escaped out the door.

"Mom is always going to be Mom. She's not

going to change at this age, you know." Evelyn said wisely.

"Yeah, I know. I'm not sure why I still expect her to. Or expect her to maybe say thanks. Or something."

Evelyn laughed. "Expecting Mother to change is like spitting into the wind, sis."

CHAPTER 3

Olivia put on a simple cotton sundress and sandals and pulled her hair back. At the last moment, she decided to walk over to Austin's cottage and grabbed a hat to keep the sun off her face. It was hot out, but she was used to the summer heat and it was nice to be outside after all the long hours she'd been putting in at the cafe. With a quick look in the mirror, she headed out the door.

She wandered slowly along the streets of Moonbeam, enjoying a leisurely pace without being in a hurry to get to work or be somewhere. Although she was kind of in a hurry to get to Austin's. She'd missed him while he was gone visiting his family.

She turned down Harborside Boulevard and

walked beside the harbor before taking a cut through to Gulf Avenue where Austin lived. Wanting to feel the water on her toes, she crossed to the beach to finish walking the distance along the shore. When she got to the water's edge, she took off her sandals and walked in the shallow, frothy edge of the waves. A delicate purple shell caught her attention, and she reached down to scoop it up, rinsing it off in the foaming water. She slid it into her pocket.

She briefly wondered how many millions of shells she'd collected in her life. She couldn't help herself. They seemed to call to her, and she had to rescue them. It was about time to find yet another glass bowl or vase to hold her growing collection. She also had some of her favorite shells scattered on the windowsill of her house. Some women could never have enough shoes... but for her, it was never enough shells. Or sea glass, but there wasn't much sea glass to be found around Moonbeam Bay.

Austin stood on the deck to his cottage and waved when he saw her. He climbed off the deck and jogged down the beach toward her. "I saw you pick up a shell, you know."

"Busted." She slipped it out of her pocket

and showed it to him. "How could I not pick it up? See those pretty lines of purple on it?"

"I'm sure you needed it. There's a severe shortage of shells in your house," he teased her.

"I'm thinking you need a big glass bowl of shells at your cottage."

"I know someone who could help me fill it." He snagged her hand as they continued down the beach toward his house.

They climbed the stairs to the deck, and she settled onto a glider, lifting her hair off her neck for a moment. "It was warmer than I thought."

"Let me get you a drink. Tea? Lemonade? A beer?"

"Lemonade sounds great."

"I got it at the store. Who knew they have fresh-squeezed lemonade and orange juice at the market?"

She laughed. "So you don't grocery shop much, huh?"

"Fresh-squeezed lemonade was not a big seller in Colorado. Just cartons of it. But I admit, I've become a convert since moving here." Austin disappeared inside.

Since moving here. Had he really moved here? She knew he still had his condo in Colorado and went back there occasionally for work. But he'd gotten a year-long lease on this cottage, so he was here for a while, anyway. He sure didn't make any noise like he was leaving anytime soon. But then he hadn't said it was a permanent move either.

He returned with their drinks, the ice clinking against the glasses. After one sip, she knew she'd made the right decision. The lemonade was delicious, the perfect combination of tart and sweet.

He sank onto the glider beside her. "Ah, this is nice. I've missed you. Just sitting with you."

"I missed you too," she agreed. "Did you have a good time visiting your family?"

His eyes clouded slightly. "I did, but…"

"But what?" She reached out and took his hand, concerned about his troubled expression.

"But my mother isn't doing as well as we'd hoped. She's getting weak. The chemo just seemed to sap all her strength."

"I'm sorry."

"It's hard to see her like that. She was always so vibrant and alive." Furrows deepened between his eyes. "She's a fighter though. Says she'll still beat this."

"I'm sure she will," she said with as much encouragement as she could give him. Because who knows the path cancer takes with a person. But best to keep a positive outlook. "And how is your dad doing?"

Austin shook his head. "He's holding on. Tries to do what he can to help Mom. He's actually taken over the cooking and he's... let's just say he's not a very good cook. Mom doesn't have much of an appetite right now anyway though. I did find her potato soup recipe and tried to make it with her help. It turned out pretty good. People from her church are bringing them food off and on."

"I'm so sorry. It must be so hard on both of them. On all your family."

"My sister is going up there tomorrow. We're trying to work it out so that someone is up there most of the time for a while." Austin turned and looked out at the water, then closed his eyes for a moment.

Her heart clutched in her chest for the pain he was going through. She couldn't imagine watching her mother go through that. Imagine worrying that her mother wouldn't be around for long. Cancer was such an ugly, unforgiving disease.

He opened his eyes and turned to give her a weak, sad smile. "Ah, we can only do so much.

Life throws us curves. Challenges. I just wish I could take some of this away from her."

"I know you do." She squeezed his hand.

"Life is short and we're not guaranteed anything. I'm really glad that I found you, Livy."

"I'm glad you did, too."

He leaned back and threaded an arm around her shoulder, pulling her next to him. "And I'm happy to just be here sipping lemonade—really good lemonade—with you."

She leaned her head on his shoulder, thinking there was nowhere she'd rather be either.

CHAPTER 4

Olivia hurried through the morning crowd at the wharf and waved to Heather, sitting at a table at Brewster's with two cups of coffee. She hadn't had time to meet her cousin for their morning coffee in far too long. She walked up and reached for the offered coffee. "Thanks."

"I think you make sure I get here first so that I buy the coffee each time," Heather teased.

"Not true. I bought it..." She frowned. "I can't remember the last time I got here before you. But I'm not late... you're just becoming a person who gets places early."

"Guess so."

"So, how is Blake?" She dropped her purse beside her and settled into her chair.

"He's settling in nicely. He loves working at Parker's. I'm not sure if he likes working at the store or the cafe more. He loves it when Emily is working the same shift as him. And she's introduced him to so many friends."

"Emily loves having a cousin. Second cousin. Whatever. They've become great friends." Livy blew on the coffee, waiting for it to cool down a smidge.

"The legal stuff is taking time. It's all very complicated. But Blake's aunt seems glad to not have the responsibility of raising him. And Jesse is so excited to have Blake living with him." Heather frowned slightly. "I sometimes get a bit jealous, you know. The two of them are getting so close. I feel... a little bit left out."

"You and Jesse worked things out, though, didn't you?"

"We did. But it still isn't like before. I feel like there is still this small layer of *something* between us."

"Have you and Jesse gone on a date since Mom's wedding? I mean, that wasn't a date, but that's when you guys worked things out."

"No, it's kind of awkward. Blake is here and we don't want to leave him sitting at home while we go on a date. Jesse did ask me over for dinner a few times with him and Blake. That's been nice."

She looked at Heather and shook her head. "I still can't believe you had a baby and didn't tell me. I would have been there for you."

"I know. I just… did what I thought was best at the time. Put him up for adoption. But now look at things. We have a chance to get to know Blake. And if things go as planned, Jesse will adopt him once all the legal stuff gets sorted. But it's all so up in the air right now."

"You probably just need to give it some more time. Let it sort itself out."

Heather sighed. "I know. I just don't like it when I feel out of control of things. Out of control of my life."

Livy laughed. "That is something we all know about you. But sometimes life just doesn't let you control things." She thought about Austin and his mother.

"What? You looked sad for a moment." Heather set down her coffee cup. "What's wrong?"

"Oh, it's Austin's mother. She's going through cancer treatments."

"Yes, you told me."

"Well, she's getting really weak, and he's worried about her."

"I'm sure. It would be so hard to see your mom like that."

"That's what I was thinking. He's just… sad. And I'm sad for him, if that makes any sense."

"Of course it does. You care about him. You feel his pain."

"I do care about him. I care a lot. But I have no idea where we're headed. I mean, he could decide to up and move to Michigan to be closer to his mom while she needs help. He can do his job from almost anywhere."

"Oh, he wouldn't leave Moonbeam, would he?"

"I don't know. We haven't really talked about how long he's planning on being here. We just… I don't know… date. Talk. Enjoy each other's company. We sometimes talk about the future, but nothing concrete." She grinned. "And we kiss. We do a lot of kissing."

"Kissing is good." Heather grinned. "I wouldn't mind doing some kissing with Jesse, but we haven't had any time alone. And I don't want to rush anything. We're just getting back on tenuous footing."

"I think I should have Emily ask Blake over to dinner at our house one night this week. Then you and Jesse could go on a date."

"That would be nice." Heather's eyes lit up with anticipation. "That would be excellent."

"Perfect, I'll set that up."

"Did anyone ever tell you that you are like the best cousin ever?"

"All the time." She grinned at Heather and took a sip of the now cool enough coffee.

Patricia peeked out the door, glad to see no sign of Ted. He was one complication she hadn't counted on when she moved here to Sunrise Village. So far she'd managed to avoid running into him again, though part of that was because she was avoiding going to the dining room at mealtime. But she was hungry now, and the little cafe downstairs did have very good soups and salads. She'd just go down there and grab a quick bite. It was midafternoon. There shouldn't be many people around.

She stood by the elevator until the familiar ding announced it had arrived, then slipped inside. So far, so safe. Just as the doors were closing, a hand reached in and grabbed the door, stopping its closure.

As the doors slid back open, there stood Ted with a warm smile and a twinkle in his eyes. Looking almost as boyish as he had so many years ago.

"I thought that was you." He stepped in next to her.

Not only next to her, *close* to her. She couldn't help herself, she stepped a few feet away. "I was just going downstairs to the cafe to grab a bite to eat."

"Fantastic. That's where I'm headed, too. Mind if I join you?" He looked directly at her.

Could he tell that her heart was pounding? She couldn't just sit and have a meal with him after all these years, could she? "I… ah… I was going to bring it back upstairs." A lie. She had planned on eating at the cafe. No use dirtying up her own dishes.

"Oh, join me. We can talk. Catch up." His eyes lit up with hope.

She couldn't think of a way to gracefully and politely decline. She was always socially proper. Always. "Sure, that sounds fine." No, it didn't. Not at all. She'd just eat quickly and hurry back upstairs.

They ordered their food, got their drinks, and went to a table overlooking the courtyard to wait for their meals to be delivered to them. Ted held out a chair for her. Always the gentleman. She did remember that about him.

She sat on the edge of the chair and placed her drink on the table. Thank goodness the cafe used real glasses instead of those ridiculous plastic cups. It made it a bit more discerning. She took a sip of her sweet tea, avoiding looking at him. Mostly. Ted settled into his chair, relaxed and at ease. Must be nice.

"So, tell me what all has been happening in your life since I last saw you," Ted said with a congenial, chatty tone in his voice.

"Oh, the normal things." Okay, she could be civil. And socially polite.

"And what's normal things for you?" He gave her an easy smile.

If he thought his amiable smile would disarm her, he was so very wrong. She didn't really feel like chatting about her life, but she couldn't think of a way to avoid at least saying *something*. "Well, I moved here from a retirement center in Naples after things went downhill there. Bad management. So a few of the ladies and I heard about Sunrise Village and we've all moved here."

"That's nice to have friends here. And it must be nice living close to your daughters."

"Ah, yes. It is." Not that she saw her daughters much. And if they kept embarrassing her with their mistakes that the whole town gossiped about, she'd see them even less. But that didn't sound very motherly, so she didn't explain *that* to Ted.

The server came and brought their meals. On nice plates. Not the china that they used in the dining room, but acceptable nice white plates. She poured a tiny bit of dressing on her salad—she always asked for dressing on the side. Some people wanted to drown salad in dressing. She couldn't abide by that.

Ted attacked his meal—a whole sandwich and bowl of soup—even though the cafe offered half sandwiches and half salads and cups of soups, which were much better portion sizes as far as she was concerned.

"So, did you ever have any children?" It was her turn to ask *him* some questions. Just so he'd stop asking her questions. Not because she was curious or anything like that.

"No, we never did. Bianca got sick. It was a long illness. She passed away many years ago."

"I'm sorry."

He nodded. "I heard you recently lost your husband."

"Ah, yes. I did. Not too long ago."

"I'm sorry to hear that. It's an adjustment, isn't it?"

How to answer that? It had been an adjustment. Nelson had taken care of so many of the details of their lives. Not to mention all the bills and finances. She was still sorting all that out. It was actually rather annoying to have to deal with all the little details now, but it couldn't be helped.

And Nelson could be... difficult. A very critical man. She was embarrassed to admit to anyone—well, she probably wouldn't *ever* admit it—that it was a bit freeing to not live under his critical eye and constant judgmental remarks.

Of course, she couldn't tell Ted all of that. "Ah, yes. An adjustment. It has been." That was a much safer answer to his question.

"And the friends you've moved here with? That must be nice to already know people here."

"Yes, I suppose it is. We went on a world cruise just a bit ago. Just these women. We were all widows or divorced. We had quite a great time of it."

"That sounds nice."

It had been nice, but exhausting. Honestly, that many days stuck together with that many people on the tour had almost been too much. She'd been glad to get back home. But then she'd had to deal with this whole move thing.

"Have you gotten all unpacked and settled in?" Ted asked yet more questions.

She let out a long sigh, releasing her frustrations with the whole ordeal. "Mostly. The concierge found me some help and they did get things unpacked. I'm not sure everything is where I want it, but it will do for now."

"It takes a while to get used to living in a new place, doesn't it?"

She just nodded to avoid saying 'ah yes' again, which seemed to be her preferred phrase today.

"Sunrise Village is nice, though. And it's nice being back in Moonbeam. I didn't realize how much I missed it until I returned. And the harbor walk. I'd forgotten how much I love the harbor walk. The town has done a great job keeping it looking nice. I've been taking a walk along the harbor every morning since I got here."

That answered her wondering the other day if he jogged anymore. But a daily walk was still more exercise than she got. Or was interested in.

"You should join me some morning." He looked hopeful.

"Ah, yes. I mean, no. I'm not much of a morning person." Or a get-out-and-exercise person.

"I remember that about you. I wasn't sure if you'd changed."

"No, I'm still the same." Though, she wasn't. She wasn't anything like the person who had been friends with him all those years ago. Not anything. Couldn't he see that? And he was probably very different than the young man he'd been back then.

With that thought firmly wrapped around her, she stood, eager to dismiss the conversation and end the lunch. "That was lovely catching up with you." *Was it really?*

"It was. Maybe we'll do it again soon."

She just nodded.

No, she didn't think that they would. She was just going to keep on avoiding him as much as possible.

CHAPTER 5

That evening, Patricia stood in the lobby waiting for her friends so they could all go into the dining room together. As her luck would have it, Ted walked into the lobby and waved to her.

"Who's that?" Betsy whispered loudly.

"A... friend."

"Well, invite him to join us for dinner."

"No, I—"

Betsy waved Ted over to them. "Hi, I'm Betsy. I hear you're a friend of Patricia's."

"Ted Cabot." He held out his hand and took Betsy's in a quick handshake.

"Oh, Cabot. Like the hotel?" Betsy's eyes lit up.

"Yes, like the hotel. My family used to own it before Delbert Hamilton bought it."

"Fascinating." Betsy took Ted's arm. "You should join us for dinner."

"I'd like that. I haven't met many people here yet."

"Then you must. I insist."

Her plan to avoid Ted hadn't lasted long...

And Betsy was ignoring her glares.

She trailed behind Betsy and Ted, none too pleased. Not pleased that Ted was joining them and... *well*... not pleased that Betsy was hanging on Ted's arm.

They had a table of six and Betsy sat next to Ted. Patricia sat across from him trying to ignore him. Not that she was very successful. Ted chatted with all of the ladies, and before the dinner was over, they all were acting like they'd been best friends for years.

Ted finally rose. "Thank you ladies for asking me to join you. It was a thoroughly enjoyable meal. Enjoyed getting to know all of you."

"You should join us anytime. We usually meet in the lobby at six." Betsy gave Ted a flirtatious smile suitable for a teenaged girl crushing on the football quarterback. The woman had no shame.

"I just might do that."

"And tomorrow at three we're meeting to play croquet. Would you like to join us?" Betsy asked. "The croquet area is shaded by then."

Would the woman ever quit inviting Ted to join them? She was going to have to talk to her. Explain that it just… It just what? It made her uncomfortable? She wasn't about to admit *that* to anyone.

"I'm afraid I have an appointment tomorrow afternoon, but I'll see if I'm back in time to join you for dinner."

"That would be wonderful," Betsy gushed.

Really, could she be any more obvious?

Ted nodded toward all of them, turned, and headed out of the dining room.

"Where have you been hiding him?" Betsy asked, watching Ted's every step.

"I haven't been hiding him. And really, do you need to ask him to do everything with us?" She glared at Betsy.

"I do believe I do." Betsy grinned, ignoring the glare. "Such a nice man. A Cabot."

Patricia knew that look. Betsy had set her sights

on Ted, hoping he'd be another in a long string of rich boyfriends she always seemed to acquire. At least until she tired of them, or they tired of her.

She'd had enough of this nonsense, so she stood. "Good night. I think I'll turn in early tonight."

She left the dining room but walked ever so slowly through the hallway and the lobby so that she wouldn't run into Ted. After checking out the lobby carefully, she didn't spy him, so she hurried to the elevator, relieved.

"Well, hello again."

She spun around to find him standing right beside her. How did he do that?

"Headed up for the night?" He asked.

"Yes, thought I'd make it an early night. Sit and read for a bit."

"Do you have time for a nightcap before retiring? We could sit out and watch the sunset on my balcony."

"I… ah."

"That's okay if you're too tired."

She wasn't a bit tired. She was… annoyed. Annoyed that Ted kept popping up. Annoyed that Betsy was shamelessly flirting with him. Before she could stop herself, she turned to him. "That sounds nice. I have time for a quick one."

What had she just said?

She'd said she would go to his suite and have a drink? Whatever possessed her to say that? What happened to her resolve to keep on avoiding him as much as possible?

Ted was a bit shocked that Patricia accepted his offer. If he didn't know better, he would have thought she was trying to avoid him. Or maybe he *did* know better. Maybe she was trying to avoid him. But she'd said yes, so that was all that mattered.

They stepped off the elevator and walked down the hallway to his suite. He opened the door and stood back to let her enter.

She squeezed through the doorway keeping as much distance between them as possible. He held back a sigh. He wished more than anything that they could get back on friendly footing again.

Determination surged through him as he followed her inside. She paused in the main room and looked around. "This is nice."

"Thank you. I was able to bring my favorite leather couch and recliner. A bit masculine, I guess, but very comfortable." He glanced around the room and realized the whole room was very masculine, but very him. A large picture of a sailboat on the harbor hung over the couch. The walls were painted a subdued paper-bag beige. It wasn't like the light and airy coastal decor that most people had here, but it suited him just fine.

She took a few more steps and turned to him as if waiting.

"Oh, yes. How about a glass of red wine? Does that sound good?"

"That sounds lovely," she answered very politely.

Most of her answers were polite. Overly polite. Like he was some kind of stranger. He wanted that to change...

He poured them both a glass and they went out to the balcony and sat in the wicker chairs with plump cushions that his niece, Cassandra, had picked out for him. Those had been bought new for this place. He loved sitting out here and watching the view or reading.

Patricia leaned back in her chair with her legs precisely crossed and her shoulders stiff. He wished she could relax a bit.

"So, your friend, Betsy. She's quite the character, isn't she?"

"She… ah… she seemed quite taken with you."

"Really? Well, I'm afraid she's not really my type. She's very friendly. I certainly appreciated the invitation to dinner and the chance to meet your friends, though."

"She's not your type?" Creases furrowed Patricia's brow.

"Oh, she's charming. Don't get me wrong. Just a little too… chatty and…" How to say that the woman was a bit too eager and seemed to be on the prowl for a man? But that sounded rather presumptuous of him.

"You mean she's obviously out collecting well-off men like other women collect shoes?" She raised an eyebrow.

He laughed. "Something like that." He was almost certain Patricia was glad that he wasn't interested in Betsy. Hm…

"What made you decide to move back to Moonbeam?" she asked.

Was it possible she had relaxed a bit? Ah, maybe they were going to be able to sit and talk with ease. "I just feel like Moonbeam is home. I wanted a smaller place, without so much upkeep. And it's nice for other people to take care of things like maintenance or meal prep when I don't feel like making a meal. Though, I admit I do like to cook."

"You cook? That's surprising. I don't picture you as a cooking person."

"It's a skill I picked up in the last ten years or so. Though it's not that much fun cooking for one. My niece, Cassandra, comes by some and I cook for her."

"I remember her from when she was a young girl here at the hotel."

"Yes, she's all I have left of our family now. The last of the Cabots, I'm afraid. Kind of sad to think about. But neither she nor I ever had children."

Patricia got quiet and looked out at the harbor, a sadness coming over her eyes. He hadn't meant to do that. They had seemed to be getting along quite nicely. He quickly changed the subject. "So, The Cabot Hotel. It looks wonderful now, doesn't it? Delbert Hamilton did a wonderful job restoring it. It does my heart good to see her full of people and all nice and sparkly now."

"I suppose he did do a good job with it. I

noticed he kept it very much like it had been before."

"Only restored and nicer," he laughed. "And tell me about your girls." He kept up with what he hoped were more cheerful subjects.

"The girls. Well, Evelyn is a cook for the cafe in Parker's General Store. A cook." Patricia shrugged with an obvious look of disapproval. "She had such potential. But then something happened and her husband divorced her. I tried to get her to work things out, but she didn't listen to me."

He remembered that about Patricia, too. She had definite ideas about almost everything and everyone. Charming and a bit exasperating at the same time.

"Donna runs the general store. I've suggested she sell it. The property alone on Magnolia Avenue would be worth good money now. But she insists she likes running the store. Works ridiculous hours. Her daughter, Olivia, works in the cafe. And Evelyn's daughter... she draws or something. An artist. Not sure how a person can make a living at being an artist, but apparently she does."

"It sounds like they are all doing well, then."

"I suppose so."

He took a deep breath. "Do you ever——"

She looked at him directly when he paused.

"Do you ever think about that summer? The one when we became friends?"

"Oh, that was so many years ago, Ted. A lifetime ago."

"I think about it," he said softly. "You were so easy to talk to at a time when I really needed a friend."

She turned from him and stared down at her glass for a moment as if looking for answers. She finally looked up at him again, her eyes full of something he couldn't quite place. "I guess I needed a friend then, too. Someone who listened to me. Who didn't criticize me and want me to be someone I wasn't."

He reached over and took her hand, not quite sure if she'd pull away or not. Instead, she stared down at their hands, not moving. "It was a magical summer for me. Even if I have a few… regrets."

Her eyes tinged with that sad look again. "Ah, yes. Regrets." She set down her glass. "I should go. It's getting late and I'm tired."

"Of course." He jumped up and followed her through the apartment.

She paused at the door. "Thank you. It was enjoyable." That overly polite tone again.

"We'll do it again sometime. Soon."

She just nodded and headed out the door. She walked to her door, turned and gave him a little wave, and slipped inside her own suite.

He shouldn't have brought up the past. Things had been going so well tonight. It was one more mistake in a line of mistakes he'd made with her. Loneliness drifted over him as he closed the door. He'd lived alone forever and quite adapted to it, so the loneliness surprised him. He wandered back out to the balcony lost in thoughts and memories and regrets.

Patricia walked through her condo without even turning on the lights and went to sit on a chair by the window. Memories cascaded through her, over her, around her. So many memories that she'd refused to let anywhere near her conscious thoughts.

Until now.

Unable to stop the flood of memories, she sat and let them wash over her. Ted had been an unexpected friend all those years ago. She couldn't even really remember how it started. She'd been to The Cabot for a luncheon with friends and gone out to sit on the deck overlooking the harbor before heading home. She spilled her drink and Ted came over to pick up the broken glass. She'd been so embarrassed. So not herself. She wasn't the kind of person who spilled drinks.

But he'd been nice and generously offered to get her another drink, on the house. When he brought the drink back, he sat in a rocking chair beside her. They chatted about The Cabot. And who knows what else. All she knew was it was hours later when she finally headed back home.

Then she ran into him at a charity event the next week. An event Nelson had refused to go to because he didn't think it was important enough for him to spend time going to. Which really meant that he didn't think *significant* people that he needed to schmooze would be there.

Or maybe… it just meant he wanted the night to himself to do who knows what.

Only she did know what. He'd been seeing someone again. One of a string of women. She remembered when she found out about the first one. She'd been angry. Indignant. They'd had quite a row, and he swore it was a onetime thing.

But as the years crept by, she realized that it wasn't a onetime thing or only one woman. But it wouldn't do to divorce. She couldn't. Not with the gossip around town and the ugliness of a divorce. So they'd found a kind of dance to their marriage. More like a side-step. They attended the functions together that he wanted her to attend. She found her own interests. Bridge with the ladies at the club. Some events at the art museums in Naples. A book club.

And so, she'd been alone at that charity event. She couldn't even remember what charity it had been. And Ted had been there without his wife. He'd said she was traveling around Italy, visiting family.

So they'd chatted again. Most of the night, if she remembered correctly. Then she'd left and gone home, only to find a note from Nelson that he was out until late. When she got up the next morning, Nelson still hadn't returned. It wasn't the first time, and he was getting more and more obvious about his dalliances. He finally came home while she was having her second cup of coffee and offered not a word of excuse. He showered, changed, and went off to work.

Anger had bubbled through her as she

finished her coffee. Evelyn was busy learning her colors with the nanny. Nelson had insisted they have a nanny, that it was just what was done in their circles. And, truthfully, the nanny intimidated her. She knew so much about raising children, teaching them.

So, she decided to go have lunch at the Cabot that day. Alone. After all, why should she sit at home getting angrier and angrier at Nelson and his…betrayal? She treated herself to a nice lunch and an expensive glass of wine. Then she'd gone shopping. Might as well rack up charges on his credit card as her revenge.

Her thoughts drifted back to now, and she rose from her chair. No more reminiscing. Not about Ted. Not about Nelson. It did her no good. It solved nothing. She headed to her bedroom to call it a night, hoping that dreams wouldn't haunt her while she slept.

CHAPTER 6

Cassandra Cabot looked up as the driver pulled up the long driveway to The Cabot Hotel. The sight of it still made her heart trip and brought an automatic smile to her face.

Her beloved hotel. Even if it wasn't *hers* anymore. Not her family's. But after growing up and living here for so many years—although it had been a long time ago—it still felt like home to her.

She climbed out of the car and paid the driver, thanking him when he handed her the new suitcase she'd just bought with swivel wheels. So much easier to tote around on her travels. And she hoped to make many trips back to Moonbeam now that her uncle lived here.

On the wide front steps, she stood for a moment and looked up at the large front door. All those years ago when she'd lived here, she'd mostly used the side access door to her family's living quarters. A spacious corner unit on the bottom floor with views out to the bay.

But no more. Now she was just like any other guest. Arriving by the front door and getting whatever room was given to her. She'd requested a room with a view and wondered which room she'd get. It was silly, but she'd always had her favorite rooms. Maybe, by some luck, she'd get one. She tugged on her suitcase and entered the lobby.

The lobby had been refurbished and looked exactly like it had for all the generations her family had owned it. Until one too many storms and the resulting damage had been all too much for her father. Too much expense to repair it and maintain it. And by that point, he didn't really have the heart to run it anymore. Her mother had died by then, and it seemed like her father needed to escape. Which he had. He'd closed the doors and traveled the world until he passed away a few years ago. More than a few years, really. Maybe five or six?

She felt slightly like an orphan, though that was silly because she was a grown woman. The only family she had left was Uncle Ted.

They'd grown closer again the last few years after many years of being estranged because of some untalked-about rift between him and her father. But Uncle Ted had turned up at her father's funeral, wrapped her in a big hug, and that had been the beginning of them finding each other again. The last two Cabots.

"Cassandra, welcome. I didn't know you were coming here."

She turned to find Delbert Hamilton standing there with a surprised and welcoming smile on his face.

"It was kind of last minute. My travel plans got cancelled, so I decided to come to Moonbeam to check on Uncle Ted. I'm hoping he's getting all adjusted to his new home here. I worry because he was used to living in his big house, and now he just has that suite at Sunrise Village. It's nice, but so much smaller. I didn't want to impose by asking to stay with him." Why was she chattering on so?

"So, you booked a room here?"

"I did."

"How long are you staying?"

"About a week." She was pleasantly pleased to see his eyes light up.

"Well, let's go over to reception and make sure they give you one of our finest." He grabbed the handle of her bag. "I'll take this."

"Oh, you don't have to make a fuss. I reserved a bayfront room."

"Of course, I do. Can't have a Cabot staying in just any room." His eyes twinkled. "Though all our guest rooms are *very* nice."

She laughed. "I'm sure they are."

Delbert talked to the man at the reception desk, then turned to her. "The Bay Suite on the top floor."

"Thank you." She didn't know what to say. The nicest suite in the hotel *and* one of her favorite rooms. Well, it used to be. She wondered what it would look like now.

"Come, I'll walk you up."

She followed him to the elevator, and they went to the top floor. He led her down the hallway to the corner suite. He opened the door and let her pass by him and enter first.

She gasped in delight at the room. "Oh, Del. It looks the same as before. Only… better." It did look like before, even down to the same shade of carpet, though it was plush and new now. The same paintings she loved hung on the wall. The drapes were new, but similar to what had been here before. It all felt so familiar. Like a well-loved keepsake. "Thank you. This is so wonderful."

He gave her an easy smile. "I remember when we were kids. This was one of your favorite rooms. We used to sneak in here when it wasn't booked."

Her eyes widened. "You remember that?" The memory of those times flooded through her.

"Of course. I remember lots about our time at The Cabot. Those summers were some of the best days of my childhood."

"They were fun, weren't they?" Joy bubbled through her at the memories, at being here in this special room… at being here with Del again.

She walked over to the French doors and threw them open, eager to see her beloved view of the bay. She stepped onto the balcony and it was as if time had turned back to those days when she was young. The fresh air washed over her with that tangy, salty scent. For a moment she was frozen in time. Delbert came to stand beside her, like he had so many times before.

They stood like that, silent, staring out at the bay with the passing sailboats and a large cruiser sliding by as the past and present collided.

She sighed. "I miss The Cabot... living here, I mean. The sights, the sounds, the smells." She turned to him. "But I'm very thankful you bought her and fixed her all up so nicely. It broke my heart to see her just sitting and decaying into ruin."

"I'm glad I did, too. And I've made The Cabot my home base now. It just feels... right. I've moved into the living quarters. I think I remember that's where you and your family lived? The ones on the first floor? And Ted and his wife lived in the upper floor family quarters?"

"That's right." She nodded, wondering if he'd redone her family's living area, or kept it like it was.

"Three bedrooms is a bit more area than I need. But... well, I like it." He smiled. "Got to have some perks of being the owner."

She smiled. "Yes, I suppose you do."

"I guess I should let you get settled." He took a step back inside, then paused. "Do you think? I mean. Would you like to have dinner with me while you're here?"

"I'd like that." She nodded. She'd like that quite a bit. There was still some thread of connection between them, even after all these years. They were just kids back then when they hung out together summer after summer when he came here with his grandparents. But she'd looked forward to those weeks of summer every year.

Until things had started to fall apart. Her father and uncle were constantly arguing. Then she'd waited one summer for Delbert's return, but he never came. She'd looked at the reservations and saw that his grandparents had cancelled, and she'd been so disappointed. The magic had gone out of that summer.

"Is there a night that works better for you?" he asked, oblivious to the memories racing through her mind.

"I'll go see Uncle Ted tonight, but maybe tomorrow if that works for you?"

"It does." A glint of eagerness lit up his eyes. "Would you like to eat here at The Cabot?"

"I'd enjoy that, yes."

"Perfect. I'll arrange it. Say, six o'clock?"

"I look forward to it." She followed him

back into the suite, pulling the doors closed behind her.

"Tomorrow, then," he said and left.

She stood in the middle of the room, staring at the door. Tomorrow. She was going to dinner with Delbert Hamilton tomorrow. That almost qualified for a date, didn't it?

And she'd waited for an actual date with Delbert Hamilton for over thirty years.

Delbert strode down the hallway of the top floor, whistling under his breath. He had a date with Cassandra Cabot tomorrow night. He never thought that would happen after he'd missed his chance all those years ago. That last summer that he'd visited, he kept trying to get up the nerve to ask her out.

But he never did.

He'd been afraid to mess up their friendship. Besides, she was beautiful and funny, and he was a gawky kid, a nerd. Still, he vowed to ask her out the next summer... but his grandmother fell ill and the trip was cancelled. Then he got busy with school and work, and life moved on.

But he'd never forgotten that girl with the

red hair and the smattering of freckles across her cheeks. The girl he could talk to about pretty much anything. Those weeks he'd spent here, year after year, had been the best weeks of each year.

He didn't have a lot of friends growing up. Went to public school but didn't fit in. He always had his nose in a book, or he studied. He wasn't into group sports. But those weeks here at The Cabot, he'd felt like he belonged. Felt like he had a really good friend.

Thankfully, he outgrew his gawkiness and made some equally nerdy friends in college. Then he started working with his father at Hamilton hotels. Now he was poised to take over the whole company.

Only... he really loved what he did. The day-to-day operations of a hotel. Buying up properties and renovating them to add to the Hamilton Hotel business. But The Cabot had been more than a business deal. It had been an emotional decision. Because of his memories. The good times with his grandparents each summer.

The good times with Cassandra.

If he did take over the business and become the CEO, he'd have to spend most of his time at the headquarters. And right now, he had absolutely no desire to move and live there. He'd come to love the town of Moonbeam. Or maybe he'd fallen in love with it all those years ago.

He rode the elevator down, his mood still flying from his good fortune. He hurried to talk to the manager of the dining room. He wanted to reserve the private dining room for tomorrow night. Make the evening perfect. Or as perfect as possible.

Delbert Hamilton had a date with Cassandra Cabot. And he had to make sure to remember he wasn't that gawky, nerdy kid anymore. He was a successful businessman. So why did he suddenly feel like a schoolboy? He rolled his eyes. He just hoped he could remain cool and collected tomorrow night. Let her see this side of him instead of how she probably remembered him.

They had gone to Donna's wedding, but he'd been a bit nervous there and Ted had been with them the whole time. Tomorrow night would be just the two of them. He wanted it to be perfect.

After he arranged the reservation with the dining room manager, he'd check in with the woman who ordered the flowers for around the hotel. He wanted an arrangement of yellow roses for the table. He remembered that about Cassandra, too. She loved yellow roses. Or at least she used to…

CHAPTER 7

Cassandra met her uncle in the lobby of Sunrise Village. She grinned when she saw him standing in a group of ladies. "Uncle Ted," she said as she walked up to him.

"Cassie, so glad you came back to town. Ladies, this is my niece, Cassandra."

The women all welcomed her. One woman seemed especially taken with her uncle. Was she actually clinging to his arm? Cassandra smothered a grin.

"Well, let's go upstairs and catch up." Ted extricated his arm and led her to the elevator.

"Looks like you've made some friends." She nodded back toward the group of ladies.

"A few." He nodded noncommittally.

He led her up to his suite. She entered the room and looked around in surprise. "Look how settled in you are. I expected boxes still stacked in the corners. But you even have paintings up on the wall and not a box in sight. It looks really nice."

"I could not stand the mess. Just kept at it until I was all settled." He walked over to the bar area. "Would you like a drink? I have some of your favorite pinot grigio chilling in the fridge."

"That sounds perfect."

"I was so pleased to get your text that you were coming back to Moonbeam for a visit," he said as he turned and handed her a glass.

"After coming back here a few times this summer, it's like the town got back in my system or something. When my travel plans got cancelled and I didn't have any work to do for the charity right now, I decided to come back." She took a sip of the wine, perfectly chilled.

"How is the charity work going?"

"It's going great. We already have sponsors for the winter gala. Hoping we'll raise enough funds to provide more computers for the children's home." She was proud of the work she'd been doing. Their foundation had started a trial project of smaller group homes for foster children instead of large facilities. Each home had between six and eight kids, depending on the size of the home. They'd found some wonderful people to run the homes, and the kids got a more normal life than living in a large facility. She hoped they could expand to a few more homes soon.

"It's a wonderful thing that you're doing." Ted grabbed his drink and led the way out to the balcony. "Dinner will be ready in about forty minutes. I enjoyed having someone to cook for again."

"I can't pass up one of your meals. You've become quite the chef." She stood on the balcony and took in the view and the scent of the salty air. "I'm so glad you moved back here. You might get tired of me visiting all the time."

"I doubt that. I'm glad I moved back, too. I find I've missed Moonbeam."

"It gives me an excuse to come back regularly." She smiled at him as she sat down on a chair beside him.

"Any time. And you could stay here if you want. I've gotten the guest room all set up."

"The trip was so last minute and I wasn't sure if you'd be unpacked and didn't want to impose. Anyway, I booked at The Cabot and Delbert arranged for me to have the Bayview Suite."

"He did, did he?" Ted's eyebrows rose. "That's nice."

"It is. He remembered it was my favorite room at the hotel."

"Hm…"

"What does hmm mean?" She eyed him.

"It's a long time to remember something like that. Wasn't it over thirty years ago when he quit coming to the hotel?"

"It was." She took a sip of the crisp tasting wine and watched as a pair of gulls swooped by over the bay.

"Hm."

"Stop, hm-ing Uncle Ted." She laughed. "I was pleased he remembered, and I love staying in the suite."

"You going to see him while you're in town?"

"I, uh. I kind of have a date with him tomorrow night." She avoided her uncle's gaze and looked out at the sparkling water. But when she glanced back at him, he was grinning widely.

"You don't say."

"Enough about my life." She blushed slightly thinking about how excited she was for her date tomorrow. "How are things here with you? It's nice that you've made some friends already."

"A few. I think I told you that Patricia Beale was moving in here. Well, it appears she lives right next door to me. I've run into her a few times."

"You knew her from when you used to live here? Before you and Aunt Bianca moved away?"

"Yes, we were… friends back then. For a brief time." He nodded. "She introduced me to a group of her friends here at Sunrise and we all had dinner together last night. Some of those ladies you met."

"Like the one clinging onto your arm?"

"That's Betsy. She seems… ah… interested in getting to know me."

"I'll say. She couldn't take her eyes off of you. I don't think she was very happy that I showed up and took you away." She laughed.

"But I'm glad you're getting to know people here."

"Yes, I'm glad, too."

They went inside and had the delicious dinner Ted cooked. Lemon chicken over noodles, green bean almandine, and a chocolate torte for dessert. Better than any dinner at a fancy restaurant. He'd become a talented cook. She helped him clear the table.

"That was delicious, thank you."

"You're welcome, dear. It was my pleasure. Who knew it would take until this stage of life to figure out I'd enjoy cooking so much."

"I'm glad to benefit from your newfound hobby." She smiled. "I think I'll go now. It was a long day of travel and I'm kind of tired."

"Would you like to meet me for a beach walk tomorrow? I know how you love walking the beach."

"Oh, I'd love to. How about if we meet at the city park at nine?"

"I'll be there." He walked her to the door. "I'm really glad you came for a visit."

She hugged him. "I'm really glad to have you as family."

"So you're saying I'm your favorite family member?"

"Since you're my only one, yes." She grinned as she slipped out the door.

Delbert stood at the reception desk sorting through some paperwork. He wasn't really watching for Cassandra to return from her uncle's. He had this work to figure out. So maybe he usually did it in his office or in his living quarters, but a change of pace was good for people. Yes, it was just a bit of a change of pace, that was all.

He quickly put the papers aside when Cassandra entered the lobby. He waved to her, and she came over.

"You're working late." She nodded at the paperwork he'd piled on the counter.

"Just finished," he said, which wasn't exactly a mistruth. He couldn't work all night, could he? "Would you care to join me for a drink on the porch?"

She glanced at her wristwatch. "I could do that. I'm a little tired, but a quick drink might help me unwind after my day of traveling."

"Perfect. What would you like? I'll get it and meet you outside."

"I don't suppose you have hot tea? Something without caffeine?"

"We sure do. How about some chamomile tea? We seem to have a lot of people who like to sip a cup of it before heading up to bed."

"That sounds perfect."

He hurried to get a tray of tea for them and meet her outside. He found her sitting at the end of the deck, her shoes kicked off, watching the lights of the boats out on the harbor. He set the tray down and she poured a cup for each of them.

"This is nice," she said. "It's very peaceful out here."

"It is sometimes. Though occasionally on the weekends it gets a bit more crowded. We don't seem to attract a very rowdy crowd here though."

She pursed her lips and blew on her hot tea, then took a tiny sip. "Ah, this is good."

It pleased him that he'd had the tea she wanted and that she liked it. Evelyn had been the one to suggest adding tea to the offerings at the bar. And it had been a great idea.

"Did you have a nice visit with your uncle?"

"I did. He seems to be settling in nicely. He's met some women there. Oh, and he said a friend from his past, Patricia Beale, is living right next door."

"Patricia is Evelyn and Donna's mother."

"Right, I remember that now. I met so many people at Donna's wedding."

"She's a recent widow, I hear."

"There seem to be quite a few widows and widowers at Sunrise Village. And one woman I met was absolutely smitten with Uncle Ted." She laughed a gentle laugh. "He is handsome, and I guess she thinks he'd be quite the catch."

"Good luck to her, then?" He tilted his head.

"I don't think he's very interested in her. But at least he's meeting people. I don't want him to be lonely."

"It was nice of you to come to town and check on him."

"He's all I have now." She took a sip of the tea. "And… I can't stand the thought of losing him. Too much loss in our family. His wife. My parents. I'm just glad we got back to being close, like when I was young. I still don't know what the fallout was that made him leave all those years ago."

"Families are funny things, sometimes."

"They are." She took one last sip and put

her cup down. "I really am getting sleepy. I should head upstairs now."

"I'll walk you up."

"No, that's okay." She rose gracefully, walked down the long porch, and disappeared inside.

He sat there for a long time looking out at the harbor. Just a simple cup of tea with her. Chatting. Nothing special. But it felt special to him.

CHAPTER 8

Cassandra met her uncle at the beach promptly at nine as planned. They headed down toward the water and walked at the edge of the waves. "I wonder how many times I've walked this beach." She reached down and picked up a shell, then slid it into her pocket.

"Probably as many times as I have. Though, the hotel did keep me pretty busy."

"Can I ask you something, Uncle Ted?" She stopped walking and turned to look at him.

"Of course." He paused beside her.

"What happened between you and Dad? I know you fought a lot. But then you suddenly left."

Ted let out a long sigh. "The first arguments

were on how to run the hotel. I thought we should get investors and spruce her up some. Do some long-needed maintenance. Your father insisted it was only family. No one else could own part interest in it."

"But what made you leave all of a sudden?"

"Ah… that wasn't so much your father and me. It was Bianca."

"Really? I thought it was Dad."

Ted reached down and picked up a shell and threw it into the waves. "It was a complicated time. You see, that last summer I was here? Bianca was in Italy."

"I remember. She was visiting family."

"To tell the truth, she said she was leaving me. Wanted a divorce. She actually started filing for one. I asked her to think about it for a while, delay it."

"Oh, I had no idea." She frowned, her heart hurting for him. "But then you went to Italy and stayed together, so it worked out, right?"

"Then her mother called late that summer and told me Bianca had cancer. She found out when she was over in Italy. I couldn't *not* go to her. Even though she'd said she wanted a divorce."

"I'm so sorry."

"We ended up getting a villa, and she went through treatment. I took care of her. It was actually a very peaceful time for us. It brought us closer together for a bit."

"But?"

"But after she was better, she spoke about separating. I couldn't change her mind. So she left me again."

"I didn't know any of this. Did father?"

"Some. Not all the details, no. I never told him that Bianca wanted a divorce, and that's why she first went to Italy. I felt like such a failure for not making her happy. For not being able to save my marriage.

"We lived apart for years. She never did file for the divorce, but we lived our separate lives. Then the cancer came back. Her mother had passed away by then, and I couldn't stand to think of her going through all of it alone. I asked her to come back to the villa. She was so weak when she got there. So fragile. I took care of her until she passed away a few years later."

"I'm sorry you had to go through all of that. And do it alone. We should have been there for you."

"I could have reached out. But I didn't. I just didn't know how to mend fences with my brother, and after a time it seemed easier to stay away. But when I heard he'd died, I couldn't bear for you to go through that alone."

"I was so grateful to see you there at the funeral."

"And I'm glad we've gotten back to being family." His eyes lit up through the pain that was still etched on his features.

"I am too. Let's never let anything get in between us again."

"We won't. I promise. There's nothing more important than family."

Her phone buzzed with a text, but she ignored it. Ten minutes later it buzzed again while they made their way down the beach.

"You should get that. Sounds like someone needs you," Ted said.

She sighed, pulled out her phone, and read the texts. "Oh, no."

"What's wrong?"

"One of our big charity sponsors is considering pulling out. They want to meet with me."

"I'm sure you'll convince them to stay in."

"But they want to meet tomorrow. Before they present their final budget to their board. I'd have to catch a flight out this afternoon."

"Then that's what you should do. Come on." He took her elbow and turned her back the way they had come.

She bit her lip as they hurried down the beach. She just had to convince them not to pull their annual contributions. She had such plans. The computers for the kids. Attract even more investors so they could expand the program. Losing their biggest sponsor was definitely not in her plans.

Delbert looked up from his desk to see Cassandra standing in the doorway. He broke into a spontaneous smile. "This is a nice surprise." Then he noticed her suitcase beside her.

"I'm so sorry, Del. I have to leave. I have to cancel our dinner plans tonight."

His excitement for their night together collapsed in a heap of broken hopes as he rose and walked over to her. "Everything okay?"

"No. One of our biggest sponsors of the charity isn't sure they're going to continue with their annual contribution. I booked an early evening flight back home. I have to meet with them first thing in the morning."

Disappointment surged through him, but he put an encouraging smile on his face. "I'm sure you can convince them to continue to contribute."

"I hope so." She didn't look very confident. "I'll sure try. I am sorry about breaking our... date."

"Don't think anything of it. It's fine. We'll do it another time."

She nodded.

"Do you have plans to come back any time soon?" He couldn't keep the hopeful tone from his voice.

"I'm not sure. I'll have to deal with this and then see. If they drop out, I'll need to double down on trying to line up sponsors. It may be awhile."

More disappointment came in waves, but he still clung to his smile, hiding his chagrin. "Well, make sure you let me know when you're coming back to town. We'll try it again."

"Thanks for being so understanding. Sorry to stand you up at the last minute."

"Really, don't worry. It's fine." But it wasn't fine. He'd been looking forward to tonight. A date with Cassandra after all these years. Once again, it wasn't meant to be. Fate seemed to always throw a wrench in their plans.

She turned and walked away, and he stared after her, feeling suddenly lonely. Which was silly, of course. He was used to being alone. But why did her leaving make him feel so… lost?

CHAPTER 9

Heather met Jesse and Blake at The Sea Glass Cafe for lunch. They'd fallen into the routine of meeting there a couple times a week. She loved the simple act of sitting and chatting with both of them. It was starting to feel normal and familiar and comfortable.

And she was getting to know Blake better. She sometimes marveled that she and Jesse had created such an amazing human being.

One thing she'd say about him, though, the boy could eat. Like everything that was in reach. And yet it looked like he hadn't put on a pound since he got here.

"I'm going to have the meatloaf sandwich, chips, and a malt," Blake said after looking at the menu board above the counter.

"I'll have the same." Jesse nodded.

"I think I'll have the salad special today. Evelyn comes up with the best salads." Today was tossed salad with walnuts, apples, grapes, and raisins in a strawberry vinaigrette dressing. She hadn't had a miss with any of Evelyn's menu items.

Emily came up to their table. "Hi, Blake. I wanted to ask. Do you want to come over to our house on Friday night? Mom is barbecuing burgers for a group of us. Then we're going to the beach for a bonfire."

Blake glanced at Jesse, who nodded. "Yes, I'd like that."

"Cool. I'll tell Mom to add more burgers. You eat a ton." She teased Blake in an easy manner.

"A growing boy needs his food," Blake asserted as he grinned at her.

"Okay, I've got to run. Working over in the general store today. Grams needs help." Emily hurried off.

Heather smothered a smile. Her cousin had come through for her. Invited Blake over for the evening. Now, if only Jesse could take time off on Friday, too. Maybe she'd even ask him out.

Maybe.

She ignored her thoughts and turned to Blake. "So you're meeting a lot of Emily's friends?" she asked.

"I am. She knows like every kid in town I think." Blake shook his head. "I'm trying to remember all their names. There's like three Ashleys and two Laurens and I keep getting them confused."

"Give it some time."

"I heard more from the lawyer this morning," Jesse said. "She said that things are moving along. Blake's aunt has signed the first set of papers. It might not be long until Blake and I are legally a family. Or at least the first stage of the long legal process."

She was happy for them, but it hurt a bit to hear that the two of them would be a family. She knew it was her own doing. She was the one who'd put Blake up for adoption. And now there was no reason to change anything about the legal process Jesse had put into place, even if she wished *she* could have guardianship—at least partially—herself.

But this process Jesse had started needed to go through so that Blake felt secure. Felt like he had a home. That was more important than what she wanted. She put on what she hoped was a supportive smile. "That's great news."

"I can't wait. I'll be glad when it's all over and official. And I like living at Jesse's."

"And I like having you there."

And she was jealous of both of them... no matter how hard she tried not to be.

"So, Blake has been getting ready for school. Starts next week." Jesse leaned back in his chair, at ease, unaware of another stab of jealousy surging through her. "We got him a new backpack and the list of school supplies."

She wished Jesse would have asked her to go with them to do the school shopping. She was still missing out on so many things. She didn't blame Jesse for being careful and tentative around her, but she wanted to spend as much time with Blake as possible.

"Jesse bought me some new clothes, too. Emily came and helped pick them out. She was very opinionated about what I should get." Blake laughed.

She smiled. "Emily has definite opinions about most things. Are you nervous about starting a new school?" She'd only gone to one school district her whole life. She had no idea how hard it might be to jump into a new school with kids who had all grown up together.

"Not really. Since Emily introduced me to so many people, I already have more friends here than I did at my last school."

"I'm sure he'll do fine," Jesse said as he reached for the plate the server brought.

They ate their lunch while chatting about school and a wedding that was taking place on The Destiny. Blake was going to help Jesse that evening. She kept catching reflections of Jesse in some of Blake's expressions. A small smile pushed up the corners of her mouth as they teased each other. They had such a great relationship. She was happy for that.

Jealous, but happy.

Blake looked at his cell phone, glanced at the time, and popped to his feet. "I've got to run. I have the dinner shift here at the cafe and they asked me to come in early, so I need to head home and change. I'll see you guys later." He turned and headed out the door.

She watched his every step. "He's a great kid."

"He is," Jesse agreed.

"I'm glad things are working out legally for you both."

"I am, too. I was worried, but seriously, his aunt wants nothing to do with him. Sad. She's already planning another out-of-the-country trip. I'm hoping to get legal papers all signed before she leaves, otherwise, it will be a while." He stared at her for a moment. "You okay with all this? You look a bit... sad."

"No, I'm happy for you two."

"But?"

He knew her so well. He always had practically read her mind. Sometimes knew her better than she knew herself. She sighed. "I feel a little left out. Of Blake's life. Of your life. I thought that after Donna's wedding when we..." She paused, wondering if she should even continue down this line of conversation.

"When we sorted things out and kissed?" His eyes twinkled as he smiled at her.

"Well, yes." Exactly that. She thought things would go smoother for them. That they'd spend time together. That they'd make it back to friends. *More* than friends. But all they'd had since the wedding was just some friendly times with Blake. But there was always the reminder, somewhere in the background, that she'd given their son up for adoption without telling Jesse.

And it wasn't like she didn't want to spend time with Blake. She wanted time with him. Wanted time with the three of them. But she also wanted time alone with Jesse, too. So they could talk. Maybe grow closer. She wanted that so very much.

"I know I've been so preoccupied with Blake. How about we go out on Friday when he's busy with Emily and her friends? Just you and me? The two of us." He tilted his head to the side, waiting for her answer.

"I'd like that. A lot." He did know what she wanted, what she needed.

"Perfect. Where do you want to go?"

"Anywhere is fine with me."

"We could go to Jimmy's. Or I could make us dinner at my house."

Dinner alone with Jesse sounded like a wonderful idea. But she couldn't quite ask it. "Whatever you want."

"Okay, dinner at my house. I'll grill out."

She smiled in spite of herself. Sometimes it was almost spooky how he knew what she wanted. "That sounds great."

"Say, six on Friday?"

"I'll be there." She couldn't wait. A date with Jesse. They needed more time together to work things out. Get back on an even keel.

And she wanted him to kiss her again…

CHAPTER 10

Olivia waited at Brewster's for Heather the next morning. She'd been determined to get here before Heather and buy their coffee. She sat at the table, proudly displaying the two cups.

Heather laughed when she sat down across from her. "So, you're getting competitive, huh? Had to get here first?"

She grinned at her cousin. "Just to prove I'm not always late so you'll buy."

"To be honest, I like getting here early so I can draw for a bit." Heather reached for her cup.

"Well, you can draw after I leave. I do have to get to Parker's pretty soon. I have so much to do, and I have a date with Austin tonight. He's taking me to The Cabot Hotel."

"Nice."

"I know. We usually just grab something at Jimmy's but he said he wanted to do something fancier this time. I'm going to have to rush home from work and change into something a bit nicer than my usual. It will be fun though. I'm so glad to have him back in town."

"Wear that light blue dress you bought recently. With the tiny white stripes. It looks great on you."

She pursed her lips. She'd been thinking she'd wear her red dress, but the blue one *was* cute. "Okay, the blue one it is."

"Have you two had any more serious discussions? Like where things are headed with you?" Heather asked.

"Some. I mean, I'm crazy about him and I know he feels the same way about me. He just… makes me feel whole. Loved. Secure. And I feel like I can be myself around him and he'll always accept it. It's a great feeling."

"You two are a great pair."

"Thanks, I think so."

"I have a date with Jesse this week, too. Friday." Heather's cheeks flushed the tiniest bit.

"Great. I was hoping he'd ask you out while Blake is busy with Emily and her friends." She smiled. "A good plan, huh?"

"I appreciate that you arranged it. And I *was* glad that Jesse asked me out."

"You could have asked *him* out, you know."

"I just… I wanted him to ask me." Heather shrugged.

"It will be good for you two to have some time alone. Just the two of you. Give you some time to talk."

"I hope so. It's like we found each other again, then the next day things exploded when Blake arrived. After a while, things started to get better. But I don't know, I still feel like I'm holding my breath around Jesse. That he's going to change his mind. That he's going to be angry with me again."

"You've got to be patient. A lot has happened between you two. Then there's the whole legal ordeal with Blake going on. That has to be stressful for Jesse."

"I know. And I'm a terrible person because I'm jealous that Jesse and Blake are growing so close. I should be ecstatic about it. And I am happy for them. But gosh, I wish I was included in that."

She reached out and covered Heather's hand. "You're *not* a terrible person. I know it's hard. Everyone is just trying to sort everything out. I heard you were at the cafe with them yesterday. So Jesse is including you in some things."

"He took Blake shopping for school supplies and clothes. I've never gotten the chance to take him school shopping." Sadness crept into Heather's eyes.

"You will. You'll get to do lots of things with him. It probably didn't occur to Jesse to ask you to go with them."

Heather sighed. "I know I should be patient. I never thought I'd even ever meet Blake or get to know him. I mean, I always dreamed about it in my mind. What it would be like. What he'd be like. And it was never anything like this."

"But he's here now. You're getting to know him. And he and Emily have become great friends. He'll know so many people when he starts school next week. And he'll meet more this weekend at the annual back to school bonfire at the beach."

"I hope he fits in well and likes the school."

"I'm sure Emily will make sure he does. You

know how she is when she sets her mind on something."

Heather laughed. "You do have a determined daughter."

"She gets it from her mother," she grinned.

"I did see his transcripts that Jesse got to give to the school. He makes good grades. I'm very proud of him for that. But mostly, I want him to be happy."

"That's what every parent wants for their child. He seems very smart, and he's such a great worker. We love having him work at Parker's." She let go of Heather's hand and reached for her coffee again. "Really, everything is working out well, isn't it?"

"Yes. It is."

But there was still that look in Heather's eyes like she was longing for something. A look that was so close to the look she had when she was a young girl, longing for acceptance from her father, longing for a close-knit family life.

She hoped that at some point in life, Heather would lose that look. That she'd find what she'd been looking for all of her life.

Later that morning, Olivia pushed into Parker's General Store, balancing two boxes the delivery man had handed her outside. "Hey, Mom. Got some deliveries for you," she said as she walked up to the checkout counter. "I'll set them in the back room."

"Thanks. Did you have a nice chat with Heather?"

"I did. I need to make a point to see her more often. She's kind of—I don't know—fragile right now."

"She's got a lot going on in her life now."

Melody Tanner, one of the best hires they'd made for Parker's, came walking up to them. "Here, I can take those. I'll open them, add them to the inventory, and stock them on the shelves."

"Thanks, Melody." She handed over the boxes.

"No problem. Then I'll be back over to take over checkout duties. I know you said you had lots of paperwork to catch up on."

"Thank you."

Ethan Chambers came through the door and spied Melody. "Hi, Melody." His face flushed a bright red. There was no welcome for her or Donna. He only had eyes for Melody.

"Morning, Ethan," Melody answered as she juggled the packages.

"Here, let me help you." Ethan reached and took a package.

"Thank you. I was just headed to the back room with them."

Ethan nodded and followed her as she walked away.

Olivia turned to her mother. "So what's that all about?"

Donna grinned. "He's been coming in almost every day, getting one thing or another. I'm pretty sure he has a crush on Melody."

"I bet that's why he keeps coming into the cafe for lunch or dinner almost every other day. Melody doesn't seem to have noticed his interest, although it was pretty obvious right there."

"I think she's just still feeling her way. She was so young to become a widow."

"She was. But she sure was a smart hire for Parker's."

"She was. She's taking on more and more responsibilities as she learns more. Never misses work, always on time. And when we're not too busy, she always finds something to do. Like straighten the shelves or set up a new display."

"She seems happier these days, too, doesn't she?"

"She does. I know she had financial problems after her husband died. I think this job helped relieve some of that stress."

"Well, maybe given some time, she'll notice Ethan."

"I hope so. Or the man will have to come in here day after day buying something, hoping she'll actually see him."

"Or eat all his meals at the cafe." She grinned. "Melody's great at the cafe, too. Takes over on the few days when Evelyn isn't in. Which isn't often. I wish you could convince Evelyn to take some time off."

Her mother laughed. "She just had the same conversation with me about you. That you should take some time off."

She grinned. "I guess both Aunt Evelyn and I could say the same about you."

"What can I say? Parker women work hard."

"That we do." She turned to head over to the cafe, pleased to have a job she loved so much. It was hard work running the cafe, but she wouldn't give it up for anything.

Now, if she could only think of a way to give Melody a nudge toward Ethan.

CHAPTER 11

As usual, Patricia peeked out her door to make sure Ted wasn't in the hall before she slipped out and hurried to lock her door. She froze when she heard a door opening down the hall.

"Patricia, wait up," Ted called down the hall.

Trapped, she waited for him to reach her. "Good afternoon, Ted." She kept her tone as polite as possible. She couldn't just blurt out she was trying to avoid him.

"I was just headed outside for a walk. It's a beautiful day. Care to join me?" He gave her his impossibly charming smile which she promptly ignored.

"I was just going down to grab a bite to eat at the cafe."

"Fine, I'll join you while you eat, then we could walk. I'll get some tea."

Now what was she supposed to say? He looked so friendly and... *hopeful*. She smothered a sigh and nodded. "That sounds nice." But truthfully? It sounded awkward and the last thing she wanted to do.

They headed downstairs and as they passed the reception desk, the assistant director came up to her. "Mrs. Beale, we really wish you'd wear your name tag when you come down here for the first month or so. Let all the workers and other residents learn your name." She could hear the mild chastising in the director's voice.

She refused to lower herself to wear the name tag. It was a nuisance to remember to put it on. And it might snag one of her nice sweaters. She'd seen people wearing theirs on a lanyard, but that was even worse. Like a bad piece of costume jewelry or something.

"I'll try to remember." Though she wasn't going to try very hard. Ted had his on. But he was a rule follower. At least, he had been. Though even rule followers sometimes bent or broke the rules...

They went to the cafe, and she ordered her regular cup of soup and half a sandwich. The food was really good here, she had to admit. Better than she'd expected. Much better than the food at her prior retirement place in Naples.

Ted chatted while she ate. Talked about his visit with Cassandra, the weather, and a shuffleboard competition here at Sunrise that he'd entered.

She began to relax as his easy conversation flowed around her. She really should get used to seeing him. He did live right next door to her. They were bound to run into each other all the time here at Sunrise. And he was a pleasant man. Handsome even as he'd aged. Not that it made any difference to her, of course.

"You're staring at me." Ted interrupted her thoughts.

"I… what? No, I wasn't." Though she probably had been.

He grinned at her. "Okay, whatever you say." He took a drink of his tea and the ice cubes rattled around in the glass.

He so flustered her, and she did not like that feeling. She liked things to be in her control, go as planned. And she had never planned for Ted Cabot to come back into her life. Ever.

"Patricia, I wish you could just relax around me. That we could be friends." He looked directly at her, a coaxing expression on his face.

"I don't know what you're talking about. I *am* relaxed."

He glanced over to where she had clutched the napkin in her hand. She set it down nonchalantly and smoothed it out.

"And we're going for a nice walk now, aren't we? Friends take walks." She sounded addled. What was wrong with her? She placed a deliberate, careful—but not too friendly—smile on her lips.

"They do. Are you ready?"

"I am." She rose and followed him out through the French doors that led to the courtyard. They walked down the sidewalk under the palm trees and past the gurgling fountain with hibiscus plants surrounding it.

She appreciated how Sunrise's grounds were so well kept up with workers carefully trimming bushes and cutting off dead palm fronds. There was the annoying noise of the lawn mowers that started at nine a.m. every Tuesday—did they have to start so early—but it really was a beautiful, well-cared-for place.

She walked beside him, and he led her down to the harbor. They walked under an old live oak tree that stretched its branches in all directions, blocking the direct rays of the sun. "Ah, this is nice."

"Oh, are you too warm? The shade does feel good. Why don't we sit?" He pointed to a bench under the tree.

They sat there, and she looked out at the harbor, *not* at him. She refused to be caught staring at him again. He stretched out his legs, relaxed yet again. How did he do that? Did he not feel even the least bit uncomfortable around her?

"Do you want to talk about it?" Ted asked casually.

"Talk about what?" She glanced over at him, afraid of his answer.

"Our past. What happened." He looked directly at her, holding her gaze.

She broke the connection and looked away. "I think it's always better to leave the past in the past." She looked down and picked a speck of dust off her slacks.

"You were a good friend to me that summer. I needed a friend then."

She looked at him, deep into those remarkable green eyes of his. "And you were a friend when I needed one. But... well... we shouldn't have been friends. It was... wrong."

"Probably." He nodded with a tiny shrug. "But I know that you were the only reason I survived that time in my life. Bianca was in Europe. She'd wanted a separation and was talking divorce. I was reeling."

She nodded. She remembered how lost he'd been, his world shaken.

"Then there was the constant battle going on with my brother about the hotel. How it should be run. The finances." He reached over and took her hand in his. "I needed someone who... liked me. Who liked me for who I was. Who didn't argue with me all the time."

She stared down at her hand in his. Feeling the connection to him. *Ignoring* the connection to him.

"But then you left. Suddenly. Just like that, you were gone."

"Yes, when I found out Bianca was very ill. I had to go to her. To help her."

"You left to go to Bianca?" She frowned. "But you didn't say anything. You just... left."

His eyes widened in surprise. "I wrote it all

in the letter I left for my brother to give you. I explained."

Patricia shook her head. "I never got a letter."

Ted's eyes flashed. "He didn't give it to you? He swore to me he would." Tiny spots of red highlighted his cheeks. "I should have known. He was so angry at me when I left. I shouldn't have trusted him."

He reached for her other hand. Now she stared down at both her hands gathered in his, still ignoring the connection. Or trying her best to pay no attention to it.

"I'm so sorry. I thought you'd gotten the letter where I explained everything. Why I had to leave so suddenly. And honestly… I knew I couldn't tell you in person. It would have been too hard to leave. To walk away from our friendship and go off to Italy so uncertain of what my future held there. You were familiar, and constant, and accepting. I don't know if I could have looked at you and walked away. But I did what I thought I had to do. I felt it was my responsibility to go care for her. She was still my wife, even if she didn't want to be at that point in time."

All these years she'd wondered why he'd

just... left. Without a word. She thought maybe he'd left because he didn't want to see her again. That they'd made a mistake becoming friends. She had heard some rumbling that he'd gone off to Europe, but that's all she'd known.

"So you got back together with her?" And was that twinge she felt jealousy? But why would that make her feel jealous?

"I did. I took care of her. She got better. Then... she left me again."

"She didn't." Patricia was appalled. How could that woman keep doing that to Ted? He was such a good, kind man. Look at all he'd done for her. Given up for her.

"She did. I know I wasn't the right man for her. I couldn't make her happy. But... she got sick again later on, and I insisted she come back to live with me. Her mother was gone by then, and she didn't really have anyone else to care for her. I took care of her until she died."

"I'm so sorry. That must have been so hard."

"You know, I've never really told anyone about what happened between Bianca and me until this week. And now I've told Cassandra, and I've told you. The two people I most trust."

He still had her hands in his and, much to her surprise, she had no desire to remove them. "Well... maybe..." She looked at the sad expression on his face. "Maybe we could find our way back to being friends. I've never had a friend quite like you. You always listened to me. And didn't criticize my every move. You were... you were exactly what I needed that summer, too."

He squeezed her hands, then let them go, a pensive smile on his features. "Friends. I'd like that very much."

And much to her surprise yet again, she thought she'd like that very much, too.

Ted stood on his balcony, a whiskey on ice clattering in his glass. He felt suddenly lighter after talking to Patricia. The secret he'd hidden from everyone about Bianca was now out there with both her and Cassandra knowing. The way he'd let Bianca just come and go as she pleased. Still, he'd been there for her when she needed him most. He'd never been able to say no to the woman. She'd been wild and free and had mesmerized him. As well as broken his heart. Over and over.

But eventually, she'd lost everything. Lost her fight. Lost her life. The brilliant light and energy that had been Bianca was gone.

And, to tell the truth, he still missed her. Even though they'd had a rocky, tumultuous existence. She was a person it was hard to stay mad at. She swept you back up into her swirl of life.

Until she didn't.

Maybe that's why he and Patricia had become friends all those years ago. She was stable. Reliable. Quiet and strong. She hadn't wanted him to change or be someone he wasn't. He wondered how many hours they had talked that summer. It seemed endless. Though, really, neither one of them had been free to become so friendly with each other. He hadn't really felt free, even though Bianca had said she wanted a divorce.

But that one summer, it was like time had frozen. The outside world didn't matter. He and Patricia had been there for each other.

And now… what would happen now? Could they really get back to how they were? Were they even still the same people now, all these years later?

All he knew was that he could really use a friend again now. And maybe, just maybe, Patricia could, too.

CHAPTER 12

Olivia walked into the lobby of The Cabot Hotel and looked around for Austin. She glanced down at her dress, glad that Heather had suggested wearing the blue one. It made her feel special.

It was nice to get dressed up for a change. Nice to have a night out on the town and something fancier than grabbing their usual dinner at Jimmy's, where half the time she still had on her work clothes.

"Hey, beautiful." Austin walked up to her and kissed her cheek. "You look lovely."

He looked handsome tonight, too. Dressed up in slacks and a button-down shirt. His hair was still a bit damp from a recent shower, and the light scent of his woodsy aftershave drifted toward her.

"I hope I didn't keep you waiting. We had a bit of a mix-up on some inventory at the cafe. I wanted to make sure Evelyn had everything she needed for the dinner rush."

"Not a problem." He took her hand in his and led her toward the dining room. A feeling of belonging swept through her with the warmth and strength of his grip He stopped at the hostess desk. "Reservation for Woods."

"Oh, yes, right this way," the hostess said.

They followed the woman through the dining room and over to a set of double doors on the side. The hostess opened them and stood back for them to enter.

"What's all this?" She looked at the single table in the room. Her favorite flowers were arranged in a vase and a set of candles flanked the vase casting delicate wavering light.

"I thought we'd take the private room tonight. The view is nice. And it's quieter in here." His smile revealed how pleased he was at surprising her.

"It's lovely, Austin. Thank you." She kissed him lightly on the lips.

The hostess closed the doors behind them, and Austin pulled her into his arms and kissed her deeply. "I've missed you."

"Since last night when we had tea out on my lanai?"

"Yes, since then. Always. Any time you aren't by my side." He loosened his arms and took her hand as they walked over to the table.

He took a chilled bottle of champagne and poured them each a glass. "It seems like a bubbly kind of night." He handed her a glass. "To us."

A warm feeling of rightness flowed through her. To be with Austin. For this night out. For the many blessings in her life. "To us."

They walked over to the window and looked out over the harbor. "This is such a great room. Delbert did a really nice job when he redid it. I heard that's the original chandelier, restored." He pointed to the lighting glowing gently above the table.

"It is really special." She gazed at the chandelier for a moment, watching it throw slivers of magical light around the room.

He took her champagne glass from her and set it on a small table by the window. "I wanted a special place for tonight." His voice quavered with the slightest, almost imperceptible tremble.

Her heart did a double beat as she stared at him. Austin was never nervous. "Austin?"

He wiped his hands on his slacks and sent her a look so full of emotion it almost caused her to stagger backward. He dropped to his knee in front of her and she gasped, holding her breath.

"Livy, I love you. With my whole heart, my whole being. And you've become my best friend." He held out a ring in a small leather box. "I want us to spend the rest of our lives together. Will you do me the honor of becoming my wife?"

She could barely hear his words over the pounding of her pulse. But she had heard him correctly, right? He wanted to marry her. Time froze in place and yet whirled around her. Marry him. Austin wanted her to marry him.

"Austin… I…" She stared at the glistening diamond. Oh, this man surprised her over and over again. Joy swirled through her.

He knelt there waiting, his eyes lit up in expectation, anticipation. Still, she stood and stared at him. Savoring every moment.

"Oh, my answer. Yes, I'll marry you. Yes." A

feeling like she'd gotten the most precious gift ever settled upon her. Her heart pounded wildly as she gazed down at him, their eyes locked, electricity snapping between them.

A wide smile spread across his face like maybe he'd gotten the perfect gift, too. He slipped the ring on her finger, then jumped up and took her in his arms. Kissing her gently. Holding her close. "I'm so happy right now, Liv. So happy."

"Me, too." She pressed her cheek against his chest and realized she was dampening his shirt with her tears but he didn't seem to mind. She couldn't help the tears, and didn't even try to hold them back.

He finally released her and handed her back her glass of champagne. "And now a toast to our future together."

She gently clinked her glass to his while her heart continued to pound. "To our future. Together." She took a sip, still unable to fully grasp the fact. She was going to marry Austin.

They turned at the sound of a knock at the door. "Come in," Austin called out.

Delbert Hamilton poked his head in the door. "Just wanted to check on things. I heard you'd reserved the private room."

"Delbert, look." She held out her hand, showing off her beautiful ring. "Austin asked me to marry him."

"He did?" Delbert stepped into the room, walked over, and clapped Austin on the back. "Good for him. Congratulations to both of you. Austin, you're a lucky man."

"I am." He nodded with a pleased-with-himself grin on his face.

Delbert chuckled. "It seems like this dining room is becoming the place to get engaged. You know your mother and Barry were engaged here, too."

She nodded. "They were." It seemed fitting that she'd get engaged here, too.

"I'll leave you two alone for your celebration. Again, congrats."

"Oh, and Delbert. Don't tell anyone, okay? I will tomorrow. I can't wait to tell Emily, and Mom and Heather."

"Your secret is safe with me." He turned and left them alone.

"Austin, this really is perfect. The room, the flowers… you." She grinned and stood on tiptoe to kiss him.

He swept her up in his arms again and twirled her around as she laughed out loud.

A surge of contentment and belonging swept through her. She was right where she wanted to be. Needed to be. In Austin's arms. Their future shone brightly in front of them, just waiting to be discovered.

CHAPTER 13

Olivia had sent a text to Heather late last night and made plans to meet her at Brewster's this morning. She couldn't wait to see her cousin and tell her the big news. A dopey grin spread across her cheeks as she stared down at the ring on her finger. She was so elated right now, like the world was showering her with radiant happiness.

But first, to tell Emily.

As if on cue, Emily wandered into the kitchen, still sleepy, and headed to the fridge to pour a glass of orange juice.

"Em, sit down. I'll make you some eggs, or what would you like?"

"Not really hungry."

"How about a bagel? I'll toast you one."

"Since when do you make my breakfast anymore?" Emily raised an eyebrow. "Most of the time you're heading out the door before I leave."

"Sit, I'll toast the bagel."

Emily plopped into a chair and sipped on the orange juice.

She cut the bagel and popped it in the toaster, then sat down across from Emily. "So... I have something to... talk to you about."

Emily eyed her suspiciously. "What is it? Am I in trouble? Everything's still on for the barbecue tomorrow, isn't it?"

"Yes, we're still good to go. It's not that. It's—"

"Spill it, Mom."

"So... Austin... last night, Austin..."

Emily swept her gaze down to Olivia's hands. "Mom. He asked you to marry him!" Emily jumped up and rushed over, wrapping her arms around her. "That's great. So cool."

"You sure? I know it will mean a big change around here. It's just been you and me... and now..."

"And now it will be Austin, too. I'm cool

with that. I'm *happy* with it. Besides I'm off to college in a few years and you'd be all alone. I worried about that."

She eyed Emily in surprise. "You worried about me being alone?"

"Of course. Like you said, it's just been the two of us for a long time. But this is great. And, he's great. And—" Emily twirled around, then plunked down in her chair. "Everything is great."

She smiled. "I'm pretty happy about it myself."

"Have you told Heather yet?"

"No, but I'm heading out to Brewster's in a few moments. Then I'll go tell Mom. I would have called her last night, but it was late. I was afraid I'd wake up her and Barry. Besides, I really want to tell her in person. So I'll go to Parker's soon."

"This is like the best news I've heard in forever." Emily jumped up and rescued her bagel from the toaster. "I'm really happy for you, Mom. You deserve this. Austin is a great guy."

"Thanks, sweetie."

Emily plopped down with the bagel and

some cream cheese and proceeded to smear the cheese on the bagel. "Now, go. I know you're dying to tell Heather. And I promise I won't say a word to Grams. You tell her when you get to Parker's."

Olivia stood and kissed her daughter on the forehead. "I'm glad you're pleased."

"Seriously, Mom. I couldn't be happier. This is great news."

Relief swept over her that Emily seemed so happy with this change in their lives. Then again, her daughter was always supportive. She'd raised a fabulous young woman. "Hey kiddo, I'm really proud of you."

Emily looked up, her mouth full of bagel. She swallowed. "What's that for?"

"I should tell you that more often. You're a great kid."

"You're not so bad for a mother, either." Emily gave her an indulgent smile. "Now, go. Quit being sappy. Go tell Heather."

Heather got to Brewster's early and sat sketching some scenes around her. A mother and her young daughter sat at a table across the deck. The young girl swung her legs back and forth, dangling them from the chair, as she sipped on hot chocolate brimming with marshmallows. Two older gentlemen sat across from each other, a chessboard between them. Each was deep in concentration. One of the men moved a piece and triumphantly called out checkmate. The other man frowned, growled, and grabbed his coffee, looking none too pleased. She loosely sketched the scene on the tablet she'd brought with her.

She was concentrating so hard that it startled her when Livy plopped down across from her and grabbed the coffee. "You beat me."

"I did. Wanted some sketching time." She put her tablet away. "So, why did you want to meet me?"

"I had something I wanted to talk to you about."

Heather narrowed her eyes. "You look… flushed. Spit it out."

Livy whipped out her hand and proudly displayed the gleaming diamond ring on her left ring finger. "Austin asked me to marry him."

She tried to squelch the automatic scream that came to her lips. She jumped up, bumping the table and sloshing coffee, and hurried around to wrap her cousin in a hug. "I am so happy for you. This is great news."

"Thanks. I'm so… well, I was so surprised. I mean, I knew we were getting serious. We made a lot of vague remarks about our future, but nothing definite. I mean, wasn't I just saying that I couldn't be certain he wouldn't move back to Denver or where his family is?"

"Guess he didn't want to do either of those."

"Guess not." Livy's lips rose into a wide grin. "Which is a good thing because I'm madly, hopelessly in love with him."

"Hey, that's always a good thing when you're going to marry someone." Heather sat back down and mopped up the spilled coffee with a napkin. "So, when are you getting married? Did you talk about when you want the wedding?"

"We talked about it. Probably about a year from now. Early fall next year. The weather here is so great then. I want to have it outside."

"At least we won't have to rush so much like we did for Donna's wedding. A year gives us time."

Livy laughed. "Gives *us* time."

"Of course. Us. The Parker women. We're going to be your personal wedding planners, you know. All the Parker women. You going to try for the pavilion like Donna and Barry?"

"I think so. It's such a lovely venue."

"I'm just crazy happy for you, Liv. Austin is so right for you." The beaming look on Livy's face made her heart sing with happiness. Who didn't love to hear such great news about their closest friend in the world?

"Thanks. I still have to tell Mom."

"Well, don't just sit there. Finish your coffee —what's left of it after I splashed it all over the table—and go find Donna. You can't just sit here waving that diamond-laden hand all around. If Donna finds out from someone else, she'll never let you hear the end of it."

Livy took one last sip of her coffee and rose. "You're right. I'm headed there right now. I can't wait to tell her."

Livy threaded her way through the tables and disappeared. Heather sat there alone with her thoughts. She *was* ridiculously happy for her cousin. She deserved this happiness.

Though a tiny bit of her was jealous. Jealous that Livy had found Austin, and they'd just…

fallen in love. No big obstacles thrown in their way. Well, none after Austin realized Emily's father, Brett, was never going to be part of Livy's life. At least not romantically.

She let out a long, self-pitying sigh. Not that she was proud of it. But it seemed like all she and Jesse had was obstacle after obstacle and really bad timing. She grabbed the tablet again. Enough of the pity party. She had a date with Jesse tomorrow. Another chance to get things right.

Olivia hurried down the wharf, anxious to get to Parker's and tell her mother the news. She kept glancing down at her ring and feeling a dopey grin spread across her face. She really needed to get her nails done if she was going to keep showing off her ring. But when would she find time to do that? She shook her head at her bouncing thoughts.

She froze when she heard her name called and saw the Jenkins twins come bustling out of a nearby shop. She started to hide her hand, but no luck.

"Olivia, dear. So good to see you." The twin —which one escaped her—reached out and grabbed her hand. Her left hand.

"Oh, what's this?" The woman stared at Olivia's hand. "Is this a *diamond*? Do you have big news to tell us?"

Olivia quickly looked left and right. "Sh. No one knows yet. I'm on my way to tell my mom right now."

"We can keep a secret," the other twin insisted as she crossed her heart.

Olivia wasn't certain of that. Not at all.

"Jackie is right. We won't tell anyone. We promise," Jillian said as she let go of her hand. The first twin had been Jillian—good to know.

"Thank you. I just need to tell my family first before the whole town finds out."

"Looks like there's going to be another Parker woman wedding." Jackie beamed, nodding vigorously. "They are the best weddings the town ever sees."

"It will be a while. A year or so."

"Well, we can't wait. We're so happy for you, dear. Now run along and tell your mother. She'll be thrilled, we're sure," Jillian swished her hands, motioning Olivia to leave.

She sent them what she was sure was a doubtful smile and hoped they'd keep the secret. Because as soon as the Jenkins twins started talking about something, the whole town found out.

She hurried to the store, paused, took a deep breath, and pushed through the front door.

"Hi, Livy," Melody greeted her.

"Hey, Melody. Is Mom here?"

"She's back in her office."

She nodded and threaded her way through the displays, to the back of the store, and knocked on the open door to her mother's office. "Mom?"

"Hi, honey." Her mother looked up with a welcoming smile.

A feeling of gratitude flowed through her. She had the best mother ever, and she couldn't wait to share her news.

"So… this happened last night." She walked over to her mother's desk and held out her hand. The diamond sparkled in the light.

"Oh." Her mother jumped up and rushed over to wrap her in a hug. "I'm so happy for you. This is great news. Great news." Her mom released her and stood back. A few tears glistened in her mother's eyes.

"He asked me last night. We had dinner at The Cabot. In the private dining room. Just like you and Barry."

"Ah, another Parker tradition is born." Her mother's face radiated happiness.

"I guess so."

"So, sit. Tell me everything." Her mom motioned to a chair beside the desk.

"It was... so romantic. And special. The room was magical. And... well, I'm so happy, Mom. We're planning on getting married in about a year. And just so you know, I ran into the Jenkins twins on the way over here. I asked them not to tell anyone... but I assume half the town will know before long."

Donna laughed. "If not all the town."

Emily poked her head in the door. "Ah, I see you told Grams. Isn't it great news?"

"It is. I'm very pleased." Donna's eyes sparkled.

"Hey, Austin is cool. I'm glad Mom found him. Or he found Mom. Or however it worked out. Gotta run. Just wanted to make sure you knew the news." Emily whirled out of the office.

"As you can see, I told Emily this morning. Heather, too. She's ready to start planning. I think she's as excited about the wedding as I am." She looked at her watch and jumped up. "I've got to get to the cafe."

Her mother hugged her again. "I'm so happy. Austin's a great guy."

She left her mom's office with her now permanent goofy smile on her face and went to tell Evelyn the news. Then she really needed to get to work. If she could get her mind back on the job, that is.

Evelyn was happy and excited, as expected. Her family was the best. Olivia settled down and helped in the kitchen until they got so busy that she went to wait tables. The Jenkins twins came in and sat at a table by the window.

"Livy, dear. Did you get a chance to tell your mother?" Jillian asked in a conspiratorial whisper.

"I did."

"Oh, thank goodness," Jackie said loudly. "I had to stop Jillian twice so far from spilling the news."

"Spill away." She laughed, knowing that now the whole town would know the news once the Jenkins twins got started. And she didn't care if the whole *world* knew she was marrying Austin.

Just then he walked through the door and came up to them. "Morning, ladies." He nodded to the twins and gave her a quick kiss on the cheek.

"Olivia told us your good news. You made a wise choice, young man. You can't go wrong with a Parker woman."

"Well, thank you, Jillian."

Olivia turned to Austin in surprise. How did he know which one was which?

"If you don't mind, I'm going to steal Livy away for a moment."

"Of course. Young love. It waits for no one," Jackie sent an indulgent look their direction.

Austin grabbed her hand and led her to the kitchen. "Hey, Evelyn," he called his greeting across the room.

"Congrats. I'm very happy for you both." Evelyn called back as she took a tray of cookies out of the oven.

She paused and shook her head. "How did you know which twin was which?"

He laughed. "I don't know. I can just... tell them apart."

"Really? I've known them my whole life and I can't."

"One of my many talents." He winked at her. "Now I have one thing I need."

"What's that?"

"A kiss." He gently reached his hand around her neck and pulled her in for a kiss. And who knew? It was precisely what she needed, too.

CHAPTER 14

Heather knocked on the door to Jesse's cottage on Friday evening, then ran her hands nervously down her hips. The yellow sundress fluttered around her knees in the gentle breeze. Maybe she should have worn the light teal blue one... And maybe she should have driven over because she was a bit warm from the walk. The heat of her cheeks made her worry she'd look flushed. She was *sure* the heat on her cheeks was just from the walk. Nothing to do with being nervous. Why should she be nervous?

The door swung open and Jesse stood there in shorts and a t-shirt. Barefoot. With a kitchen towel thrown over his shoulder. His warm smile welcomed her. "Hey there. I was just finishing up in the kitchen. Come in." He stepped aside.

She slid past him, grateful for the air-conditioning. She kicked off her shoes by his door and padded after him.

"I've got a salad made in the fridge. I'm going to grill us some grouper. Oh, and I picked up dessert from Evelyn. Peach pie."

"That all sounds wonderful. And I love Evelyn's peach pie. She uses an old family recipe. Grace's."

"It's one of my favorite things she bakes at the cafe. Though, to be honest, I haven't really had anything there that I didn't love." He reached into the fridge. "Beer?"

"Perfect." An ice-cold beer should cool her off. Maybe. Because even here in the air conditioning she felt flushed—*nervous*—which she was just barely able to admit. What was there to be nervous about? She was just having a nice meal with Jesse. She'd had hundreds of meals with him.

"Why don't you head on out to the deck? I'll be there in a minute."

She walked out and sat on the glider, glad for the breeze. She slowly drew in a deep breath.

Settle down. It's okay. Everything is okay.

Jesse came out and set the fish down by the grill. "Coals should be hot enough soon." He walked over and leaned against the railing across from her, sipping on his beer.

She sat there silently, uncertain. And yes, nervous.

Jesse grinned at her. "So... are you as nervous as I am? Which is silly, but it is what it is."

"I so am." She nodded vigorously, glad she wasn't alone in her unease.

He reached out and pulled her to her feet. "So, how about we break the ice?"

"Sure, anything."

He pulled her closer. His hand grazed her chin, tilting her face, his lips meeting hers.

She sank into his kiss, holding onto his arm with her free hand, wishing she'd set her drink down so she could wind her arms around him.

It didn't even surprise her when he took her beer from her and set it on the railing. He always knew what she wanted. Needed. He pulled her back into his arms and kissed her deeply, then a low growly sigh escaped his lips. "I've been wanting to do that for the longest time. I've missed those lips. I've missed holding you."

"Then kiss me again." She grinned up at him. "No use wasting our time now."

He threw back his head and laughed, then kissed her again. Then once more. He finally pulled away. "I really have to put the fish on the grill or we won't have dinner tonight."

Was that really such a bad thing? Dinner was overrated. As far as she was concerned they could just stand here all night kissing.

"Mom, here's more of the dishes." Emily walked in from the lanai with a tray of plates and glasses. "Thanks for letting us barbecue here tonight."

"Thanks. I'll get the rest. You and Blake go head out to the bonfire." Her mom took the tray from her.

Blake came up beside her, his hands full of empty soda cans. "Are you sure? There's still more to clean up."

"I'm sure. You two run along. The back-to-school bonfire is a town tradition. I even went to it when I was in high school. You can't miss it," her mom insisted.

"Thanks, Mom." Emily kissed her cheek. "You're the best."

"Have fun."

Emily tugged on Blake's hand. "Come on. Let's go. We don't want to miss when they light it."

They hurried down the sidewalk, and she showed him a shortcut to the beach.

"I feel like I'm never going to learn my way around town. I would have headed over to the harbor and walked along the harbor walk." Blake shook his head, and a sheepish grin overtook his features.

"Nah, this cuts off a lot. But the view is prettier that way. I do like this street, though. All the huge Victorian houses with their big front porches. Looks like a historical novel or something."

"They sure are some big homes."

"It's one of the first streets that was built in Moonbeam. Before all the canals were dredged to make all the waterfront property. And these houses have really been kept up well, haven't they?" She laughed. "Hope I'm not boring you with Moonbeam history."

He shook his head. "Not at all. If I'm going

to live here, I want to know all about it. I mean, you've lived here your whole life. You know everything about the town. I'm still the new kid."

"I'm doing my best to make sure you know everybody, too."

"No kidding. I think I've met like a million people."

She laughed. "We don't even have a million people here. We're just a small town."

"Seems like you have a lot of people to me."

They reached the edge of the beach, and she tugged on his arm. "Come on. Look, they've got the bonfire all built, but it isn't lit yet." They hurried over to the group of high schoolers hanging out on the beach.

Jeanie Francis sauntered up to them. "Hi, Blake. My dad dropped off coolers of sodas. Do you want one?" She gave Blake a dazzling smile.

"Uh, sure."

Not that Jeanie offered *her* a soda. She rolled her eyes. Couldn't she see that Blake wasn't interested in her? They walked over to the cooler and Jeanie dug into the ice and pulled out a can for Blake.

She rolled her eyes again and sank her hand into the icy depths and pulled one out for herself. They headed over to the bonfire.

"We're just getting ready to light it," Jeanie said as she stood as close to Blake as possible without actually being on top of him.

Blake took a step away, and Emily smothered a grin.

The class president did the honors of lighting the bonfire, and they all broke into cheers and applause. She loved this tradition. Loved feeling so connected to the town. She glanced over at Blake. Hopefully she could get him to feel like he belonged, too. Because he was family. And their family stuck together.

She grabbed his arm and pulled him away from Jeanie. "I want to introduce you to some more kids that didn't make it to the barbecue. When I'm done, you're going to know the whole school." Jeanie glared at her, but Emily sent her an innocent smile.

She whispered to Blake as they walked away. "Jeanie's got her eyes set on you."

"I guess."

She stopped and looked closely at him. "But you're not interested in her, are you?"

"Not especially. She's... loud. And pushy. And she said she hates school. I have to do really well in school. I'm going to try for scholarships to college. I can't get sidetracked."

"Good. Because she's not for you. There are plenty of other less—" She bit back the less charitable words that came to mind. "Less *annoying* people you could date."

Blake took it all in stride, meeting so many kids. She was certain he wouldn't remember all their names tomorrow. Jeanie was a pest and kept popping up beside him throughout the evening. Again and again.

Finally, toward the end of the night, Jeanie came up to them yet again—could she not get a clue?

"Blake, would you walk me home?" Jeanie put her hand on Blake's arm. "Please?"

Blake shot Emily a panicked look.

Emily plastered on an expression that she hoped said she was sorry—though she *wasn't.* "Oh, he can't. He promised he'd walk me home and make sure I got back okay. You know. Family obligations."

Jeanie scowled. "You surely can walk yourself home."

"No, I'm going to walk her home," Blake insisted.

"Fine." Jeanie sent her a glare and stalked off.

"I think I made her mad." Blake watched as Jeanie went over to another group of kids.

"Maybe. She'll get over it. All the guys at school that she was interested in have either dated her and got dumped or have no desire to date her. She's just looking for a fresh conquest."

"Well, it's not going to be me."

"Come on." She grinned at him. "Now you have to walk me home after making such a big deal out of it." She hip-checked him and started racing down the sidewalk. Blake sprinted to catch up, and she slowed down as he reached her. "You know, for a cousin, you aren't half bad."

"Same to you," Blake gasped out as he bent over, catching his breath.

"But I can beat you in a race."

"Competitive much?" He stood up. "Besides, you cheated and took off running before I knew we were racing."

"Gotta stay on your toes, buddy." She toyed with taking off running again but didn't really have the energy. "Hey, I've got the keys to Parker's. Wanna get some ice cream before we go home?"

"We can do that?" His eyes widened.

"Of course. I just have to make sure we lock

back up. Come on." They turned down a side street and headed to Parker's.

Jesse and Heather sat outside, sipping wine and talking. It was a perfect evening as far as she was concerned. She hadn't felt this close and connected to Jesse in... well, in a really, really long time.

He kept an arm draped casually around her shoulder and she felt right at home being tucked up against his side.

"So, what do you say, Heather Parker? You think we weathered the storm?"

"I hope so. I hope you've really forgiven me for not telling you about Blake." She sighed. "I wish I could go back and do it all over. But I can't change the past."

"You did what you thought you had to do. I realize that now. I wish we could have a do-over with Blake, too." A sadness clung to Jesse's eyes, but then they brightened. "But we have him in our lives now. We're very lucky."

"We are lucky." She was lucky. Lucky to have this second chance with Blake *and* with Jesse.

"I want to spend more time with you, Heather. The two of us. It's just hard with Blake and The Destiny and all the legal stuff going on."

"I'd like that, too. I'd also like to spend more time with the *three* of us."

Jesse pulled her close. "I'd like that. And, after the fact, I realized I should have asked you to go back-to-school shopping with us. I don't want you to miss anything going on in his life now."

"I admit, I was jealous you got to take him."

"I'll do better. Hey, you want to come over Monday morning to see him off for his first day of school?"

"I absolutely do. I'll bring breakfast from the cafe."

"Perfect. I'm a bit nervous sending him off to a new school. I hope he likes it and fits in."

"Oh, I'm pretty sure that Emily has decided he'll fit in. And what Emily decides, usually happens." She laughed. "But I'm nervous about him heading to school, too."

"Most parents have this when they send their kid to kindergarten, not high school." Jesse gave her a wry grin.

"But we missed that," she said softly as she rested her head against his shoulder.

"Hey, you need to stop beating yourself up. We missed a lot, but we'll just have to make up for it as best we can now." He kissed her forehead.

His words and acceptance comforted her. If only she could actually forgive herself someday. She wasn't sure that was possible.

"I could take your mind off your worries."

She looked up at him and he gave her a mischievous smile. "How's that?"

"I could kiss you some more."

"I think that's an excellent plan. Practical even." She struggled to keep a serious expression on her face. She lost as a smile crept across her lips.

He leaned over and kissed her gently, sweeping her hair away from her face, cupping her chin in his hand. "Ah, Heather." He sighed as he leaned in to kiss her again.

She wanted to stay like this forever. In his arms. Kissing him.

A noise at the door to the deck drew her attention away from his kisses. "Oh." She jerked back away from Jesse.

Blake stood in the doorway, grinning

broadly. "This is the best thing I've seen in forever." He laughed. "Don't mind me. I'm just going to go back to my room."

"Uh, hi, Blake," Jesse stammered.

"No, stay." The heat of a blush flushed her cheeks at being caught kissing.

"Nah, I'm tired. Had a great time at the bonfire though. Night, Heather. Night, Jesse." He turned to head inside, then looked back. "I'm really happy you two are working things out."

Jesse shook his head after Blake left. "Well, that was awkward. I feel like a schoolboy getting caught necking under the bleachers or something." Then he grinned wickedly at her. "But since he went inside, you wanna kiss some more?"

"I think I do." She nodded soberly, struggling once again to hide her smile and once again failing.

"Perfect." He leaned over and covered her lips once more.

CHAPTER 15

The next morning Jesse puttered around the kitchen, cleaning up the dishes from last night, making coffee, and waiting for Blake to wake up so he could tell Jesse about his night. Before long, Blake stumbled into the kitchen, his eyes half-open. "I've got to get to work at Parker's in an hour."

"Let me make you some breakfast."

"I think I'll just grab a bowl of cereal. If I get hungry later, I'll grab something at work." Blake went to the fridge and stared into it. "Oh, yeah, the milk." He reached inside.

Jesse handed him a bowl and the box of cereal—he was going to have to get more—then fished a spoon out of the silverware drawer. They both poured bowls of cereal and dug in.

"So, did you have a good time last night?"

"I did. I met tons more people. I thought I had met a lot already, but there were like a bazillion more there last night. I'll never remember their names."

"You'll get to know them."

"I guess. And, there's this girl. Jeanie Francis. Emily says she likes me. But... I don't really like her. I mean, not like that. She's kind of loud and flirty and... I don't know. Not my type, I guess. I kind of tried to ignore her. But I think she got mad. I don't want to make enemies when I've barely started making friends."

"I'm sure it will be okay. She'll move on to someone else, I bet."

"I guess. But having Emily as a cousin is awesome. She knows everyone and invites me to hang out with her friends all the time. At least I'll know people on my first day of school."

"That reminds me. I asked Heather to come here Monday morning to see you off to school. Hope that's okay."

Blake shrugged. "I guess so."

"I'm going to try and include her in more things we do."

"That's good. I think she wants to do stuff with us."

"She does. She wants to get to know you better."

"If she knows how to do calculus, she can be my new best friend. I have to take it this semester, and I'm not sure I'm going to be very good at it."

Jesse laughed. "Math was not Heather's forte. But helping with English, or any papers you have to write, or art. She's your girl. Oh, and history. And pretty darn good in biology."

"So, like every subject but math?"

"Pretty much." Jesse nodded.

"Good to know."

"I'm working The Destiny tonight. Want to come along and help?"

"I do if I get off work in time. I'll text you."

"Sounds good. If not, I'll meet you back here at home after we dock."

"Jesse?" Blake set his spoon down and looked directly at him, a frown on his face.

"What is it?"

"Do you think this legal stuff is going to get sorted out soon?"

"I sure hope so. But it might still take a while."

"I keep thinking that maybe it's not really going to work out. That something is going to go wrong. Because… well… this is the most I've felt like I'm—*home*—since my mom died. I feel like… like I'm part of a family again. So I'm glad Heather is going to do more stuff with us."

Jesse's heart soared at Blake's words. "We'll make sure we include her more."

Blake stood. "Thanks. I'm really glad I didn't ruin it for you two."

"You didn't. We hit a rough patch, but we're all good now."

Blake rinsed his dishes and put them in the dishwasher. "I better run. Don't want to be late for work."

And Jesse just sat at the breakfast table, a goofy smile on his face, pleased with his life right now.

Patricia and Ted had started meeting for a late lunch at the cafe most days. He looked forward to it. Gradually Patricia seemed to relax more around him. She was a bit different now, but that was to be expected. A bit… harder, tougher, or some word he couldn't quite pin down. She made some judgmental remarks about people that surprised him, but he knew she'd gone through a lot in the years since they'd been friends. Life had a way of hardening people sometimes. But she hadn't turned that side on him. To him she was always complimentary and friendly and easy to talk to.

On this Saturday they were the only two eating at the cafe. Patricia had her typical half salad and cup of soup. He was enjoying a roast beef sandwich, salad, and soup. Along with a piece of chocolate cake. The food here at Sunrise was quite enjoyable, but he was trying to get up the nerve to ask Patricia over to his suite for dinner and cook for her. But things were going so smoothly between them that he hadn't wanted to rock the boat.

He looked up and was surprised to see Donna standing by their table.

"Hello, Mother. Ted. The receptionist said I could find you in here."

"Donna, what are you doing here?" Patricia frowned slightly.

"I came to ask you—in person, so it would be harder to say no—if you wanted to come to a brunch tomorrow. It's kind of a last-minute send off to school for Emily and Blake."

Patricia's frown deepened. "I don't think so."

"Come on, Mom. You have to get to know him soon. He's a great kid."

Patricia's frown deepened even more—if that was even possible—and she looked over at him and let out a long sigh. "You might as well know, the whole town is gossiping about it. Heather has a son who she had out of wedlock. She gave him up for adoption. But now he's here in town."

"And we love him," Donna added forcefully with a fierce protective look on her face. "He's a great kid. His adopted mother died, and he came here and found Heather and Jesse. We're glad to have him here in the family."

"And you haven't met him?" Ted asked, confused.

"Briefly." Patricia nodded almost dismissively.

"But aren't you curious to get to know him? I know I would be if I found out I had a grandchild. Or I guess great-grandchild, right? I think that's great. A person can never have enough family." Even though he and Cassandra only had each other now. Small family, but he was very grateful for having her back in his life.

"It's just not right." Patricia shook her head.

And there was the judgmental Patricia coming out. Not the gentler side of her that he knew.

"Ted, you should come too. All the guys will be there. Barry and Austin and Jesse." Donna turned to him.

"I'd love to." He cocked his head and looked at Patricia, hoping she'd say yes if she had his support.

"Fine." She let out what could only be described as a long-suffering sigh. "I'll come for a bit."

"Perfect. Noon tomorrow. At my house."

"Can I bring anything?" Ted offered.

"No, I've got it covered. We'll see you two tomorrow." Donna started to walk away, then turned back. "And, Mom, I'm really glad you're coming."

Patricia watched her daughter leave, then turned to him. "I really think we should have declined."

"I don't understand that. Don't you want to get to know Blake?"

"I…" She stopped and looked down at her hands. "I guess so. It's just so… strange."

"It will be fine. You'll see."

Her look said she wasn't convinced.

"I'll be at your door at eleven-thirty. I'll drive us over."

"The whole town is talking about him. About Heather. About the family."

"Do you really care what the town talks about?"

"I don't like to be the center of gossip. Not ever."

He decided not to press on. She'd said she'd go, and he'd be there by her side. Hopefully, she'd soften up when she met the boy and got to know him.

CHAPTER 16

Patricia carefully dressed the next morning —earlier than she would have liked to be up and getting ready—in white linen slacks, a royal blue top with a draping neckline and cap sleeves, and white dressy sandals. She carefully applied her makeup and did her hair, even though she was sure that Donna would be having most of the get-together out on her lanai and the large screened enclosure around her pool. The humidity was bound to do a number on her hair. Why Donna couldn't do these family things inside like normal people was beyond her comprehension.

Her girls would be dressed more casually. They didn't do the kind of casual that she did. She did more of a country club casual and they did more of a casual-casual no matter how many times she'd tried to teach them otherwise.

She wasn't a fan of big family events, anyway. Who celebrated going back to school with a big family bash? She looked in the mirror and tucked a lock of hair back in place, and frowned. And really, she always felt a bit out of place at these things. Her daughters were close to each other. Her granddaughters were close. It was like the four of them—and Emily, too—had some kind of secret bond. When the town talked about the Parker women, she knew they weren't really including her in that group, even if she had descended from Grace Parker.

She grabbed her purse and looked at her gold watch. It had been a present from Nelson. A designer brand with delicate diamonds encircling the face. But the face was so tiny it was hard to tell time on it now without getting out her reading glasses. She still wore it because... well, it was classy and stylish.

She glanced at the wall clock. Exactly eleven-thirty. Of course, Ted was right on time. She opened the door to his knock.

"You look lovely, Patricia."

She admitted she liked the approving look in his eyes. He looked pretty great himself. He was dressed smartly in slacks and a collared knit shirt. The warm golden-yellow color of his shirt made the amber flecks in his green eyes sparkle. She forced herself to quit looking at him. "I'm ready."

They drove over to Donna's house, mostly in silence. "We'll be a bit early," she finally said. "Do you mind driving along the harbor and taking the long way? I don't really want to be the first one there."

"Of course. Whatever you want." Ted turned down the harbor road.

Nervousness swept over her. So much to fret about. Ted being around her family. They were... boisterous at best. What kind of impression would they make on him? And then there was the Blake issue.

And she wanted to make sure she held her tongue on certain things. She knew she had a way of being a bit... bristly... sometimes. But then sometimes her girls needed to be given advice. Not that they listened to her very often. Ted didn't need to hear her giving them guidance, though.

They arrived at Donna's a few minutes after noon. At least the clock in his car was readable without glasses.

Ted opened the car door for her and helped her out. Only one other car was here, but that didn't mean much. It seemed like everyone in her family walked everywhere. She took his arm, and they went up to the door.

She normally would have just entered, but now that Donna was married to Barry and he lived here, she felt it more proper to ring the bell. She pressed the doorbell and Emily appeared. "Hey, come on in. We're all outside."

Of course, they were. She fussed with her hair, knowing that the end of her perfectly done hairdo was coming soon.

They walked outside, and everyone grew quiet for a moment. Donna hurried over. "Mom, Ted, hi. Glad you made it. Ted, do you know everyone here?"

"I think I met everyone at the wedding."

"Great. I'll get you drinks. Mother, do you want a mimosa?"

"That sounds nice."

"Ted?"

"A beer sounds good."

"Okay, I'll be right back. Go over and say hi to everyone."

Patricia kept hold of Ted's arm as they walked across the slightly uneven pavers—

Donna really should have them fixed—and went to where everyone was standing by a tall table and gathered in the scattered chairs. She politely smiled at everyone in greeting.

Heather walked over to them. "Grandmother, I'm glad you came." Even as her words sounded welcoming, Heather gave her a warning look.

Blake and Jesse came up beside Heather. The boy looked at her tentatively. She nodded at him, unsure of what to say.

"So Blake starts school tomorrow at the high school with Emily," Heather stated the obvious since that was the point to this whole family party.

The family seemed to have a party for every little thing, and for the life of her she could not figure out why. Now that she was in town, she would undoubtedly be asked to more of them. An annoyance she probably couldn't avoid.

"Kind of hard to be the new kid," Ted said as he smiled warmly at Blake. "You nervous?"

"Kind of. But Emily has introduced me to about three million people, I swear." He shook his head and flashed a smile.

Emily came up beside Blake. "Not three million, but lots."

"What kind of subjects do you like most?" Ted asked as she looked at him in amazement. How did he know how to talk to *children*?

"I like science. And I'm pretty good at art."

"You are?" Heather peered at the boy with a look of surprise. "I didn't know that."

Patricia frowned. Heather didn't even know what classes the boy liked? What kind of mother — She stopped her thought. Of course Heather had just now met the boy. Truth be told, she didn't really remember which classes her girls had liked either. She'd been traveling most of the time. Her mother had taken care of the girls for a lot of the time when they were growing up. She, herself, had simply never gotten into the whole mothering thing. But look at the girls. They'd turned out fine. Fairly fine. Donna insisted on running that store that could have been long sold and brought in some good money. And Evelyn had just let her husband divorce her.

Donna came over and handed them their drinks. She took a sip of the mimosa and tuned back in to the conversations going on around her.

"Yeah, I'm pretty good at my art classes. And I'm okay at my English classes, but I still struggle a bit with calculus." Blake turned when Evelyn walked up beside him.

It was like he had his own defense team surrounding him.

"I'm sure Blake will do fine in school," Evelyn said as she draped an arm around his shoulders.

They all stood in awkward silence for a moment until Donna announced, "The burgers are ready. Let's all get our plates and fill them up."

Suddenly everyone was bustling over to the long table of food Donna had set up on the lanai. Laughter started again. Teasing. The conversations whirled around her as she got a small plate of salad.

She and Ted sat at a table in the shade with the ceiling fan above them struggling to swirl the stifling humidity. She looked over at Emily and Blake, laughing with that Jesse fellow. Donna and Evelyn stood chatting with Barry. Olivia and Heather stood with Olivia's new man... that she'd heard had asked Olivia to marry him. But she couldn't for the life of her remember his name.

"Your family is great. Must be wonderful to have such a large, fun-loving family. One that celebrates even the little things like heading back to school at the end of the summer," Ted said, then attacked his burger, slaw, and chips.

"They are rather exuberant." Rowdy, even. But that sounded like they were an uncouth group of hooligans. She picked at the salad, disappointed that the dressing was already on it and not on the side. Donna knew she liked her dressing on the side.

"I'd give anything to have a family like this," Ted looked over at the kids, laughing yet again at something Jesse said.

She looked at her watch, annoyed that she couldn't tell the time on it, and wondered how much longer they needed to stay before it wouldn't look rude to leave.

"At least Grandmother didn't say anything rude about Blake," Heather whispered to Livy and glanced over to where their grandmother was fanning herself as she sat at the table with Ted.

"No, she didn't. Surprising. I'm not sure I've heard her critique anyone or anything so far today. Very unusual." Livy glanced over at their grandmother, too.

"I find it interesting that she's hanging around with Ted these days. He seems like a nice man."

"So are you asking what would a nice man see in Grandmother?" Livy laughed.

Heather blushed. "No, not that. Not exactly. She's just…"

"Hard to be around? Hard to please? Hard to live up to her expectations?"

She sighed. "Exactly that. And I don't want her giving any of that stress to Blake. He doesn't need to feel disapproval from her." She could hear the mother-bear protectiveness in her own voice.

"Well, she's on her best behavior today. Come on, let's help Mom clear up the dishes and see if anyone wants another drink." Livy turned away.

She glanced around to see where she could start to help and reluctantly headed over to her grandmother's table. "Here, let me get your dishes."

"I could help with that." Ted started to stand.

"No, no. Sit. I've got them." Ted really was a nice man. Offering to help. Friendly. And she could not for the life of her figure out why he was seeing her grandmother. Maybe he saw a different side of her? She eyed her grandmother. Nah. With Patricia what you saw was what you got. "Grandmother, can I get you something else to eat? You hardly touched your salad."

"The dressing wasn't on the side like I like it."

"Ah… okay." She picked up her grandmother's plate. "Donna's got dessert. Actually Mom made it. Peach pie."

"That sounds delicious." Ted's eyes lit up in anticipation.

Grandmother's didn't. She frowned. "Maybe she has some fruit or something that's a bit more healthy?"

"I'll check." Heather turned away and rolled her eyes. Grandmother was always… Grandmother.

She returned with a piece of pie for Ted and some apple slices and strawberries for her grandmother. "This is all I could find."

"It will be fine." But she eyed the plate skeptically.

Ted took a bite of the pie and broke into a wide, approving smile. "This is the best pie I've ever had."

"Old family recipe." Heather was glad

someone was appreciating the meal. "And you're right, it is the best ever."

Heather headed over to talk to Emily and Blake. Someone else could do the grandmother duty for a bit. She'd had her turn and was over it.

Donna cleared the last of the food off the table and couldn't help overhearing Ted and her mother talking.

"Do you want to go over and talk with Blake?" Ted asked.

Donna glanced over to see her mother's reaction. A frown.

"No, I'm fine here in the shade." Her mother shook her head no.

"But don't you want to get to know him? I think it's so great that he found Heather and Jesse after all this time."

"I… I'm tired. I think it's probably time for us to leave."

Donna set the dishes she'd been collecting down with a clatter and turned and walked over to her mother's table. "Mother, you should try to get to know Blake. He's family." Her cheeks grew warm as she tried to control her anger. "Do not make him feel unwelcome. I won't stand for it."

"Don't use that tone with me," her mother shot back.

"Mother, keep your voice down. Seriously, we want Blake to know he's family. Because he is. Please, please go over and get to know him."

"Come, on Patricia, let's go talk to the boy for a bit. Then I'll drive you home." Ted stood and looked at Patricia encouragingly.

"I came to this party. That shows my acceptance. I don't need to go stand out in the blazing heat and carry on a conversation. I'm ready to go, Ted." Her mother swooped up from her chair. "Now."

Ted frowned. "Okay, whatever you want." He turned to her. "Donna, thank you for inviting us. The food was delicious. I really enjoyed getting to know your family better."

"Glad you could come." She stood with her arms crossed, staring at her mother. *Okay, maybe glaring.*

"Say my goodbyes." Her mother turned and glided away in a dismissive sweeping swoop and disappeared into the house.

Ted stood there awkwardly for a moment. "I'm... sorry."

"Don't be. It's not your fault. It's just Mother being... Mother."

Ted hurried away, and Donna sank into the chair her mother had just vacated. She picked up a strawberry her mother hadn't even bothered to pretend to eat and bit into it.

She should listen to her sister. Evelyn was wise *and* right. Their mother was never going to change, and it was silly to keep thinking that she would.

CHAPTER 17

Heather woke up way too early on Monday morning. It wasn't even light out. She got up and dressed.

Then changed clothes.

What did one wear to send their son off to his first day of school? Okay, so it wasn't his *first* day. But it was the first day for her to see him leave for school.

When the sun just started to lighten the sky, she headed to the cafe to pick up some cinnamon rolls. The sweet scent of cinnamon and yeast whirled around her as she entered the kitchen. Her mother greeted her. "Well, good morning."

"I came for rolls for Blake's breakfast. First day of school."

"It is. Livy is coming in late today. She wanted to see Emily off to school, too. I'll get you the rolls."

Her mother bagged up the goodies and handed them to her. "Tell Blake I wish him luck on his first day."

"I will." She headed out and over to Jesse's. She was way too early, but that was okay. She didn't want to miss anything. Jesse would be out soon to look at the sky, checking out the day, like he always did, so she went around to the deck to sit and wait.

Sure enough, soon she heard the door open behind her and Jesse's laugh. "You're up early."

She turned to see him standing in the doorway, sleep still clinging to his eyes, and a mug of coffee in his hand.

She sprang to her feet. "Didn't want to miss anything."

"Come in. I'll get you some coffee."

"That sounds great. I didn't even think to make any this morning or snag any at the cafe." She followed him inside and he poured her a mug and she placed the bag of rolls on the counter.

"Is Blake all ready, you think?" She blew on

the hot coffee, wanting it to cool slightly so she could drink it. How had she forgotten about coffee this morning? Just went to show how addled she was.

"He is. Packed up his backpack last night. Emily is meeting him near the school and they'll go together."

"She's a great kid. That was nice of her." Heather was grateful for everything Emily had done to smooth Blake's transition to Moonbeam.

"Morning." Blake stood in the doorway to the kitchen, fully dressed, his eyes bright, his backpack hanging off one shoulder.

"Good morning," she replied, and it occurred to her—surprised her—that this was the first morning she'd ever welcomed him to the day right as he woke up. Except for that single day after he'd been born when she held him and stared into his little face, in awe of him. She chased the memories away. "I brought cinnamon rolls."

"Or I can make you bacon and eggs if you'd rather," Jesse offered then turned to her. "I should be making him nutritious breakfasts before school, shouldn't I?" He raked is hands through his hair, uncertainty clear on his features.

Jesse was right. She should have been thinking of nutritional food to start Blake's day. She had so much to learn about this mother thing.

"No need to make a big deal about breakfast. A cinnamon roll sounds good." Blake dug into the bag and took out a roll, taking a big bite out of it.

Jesse poured orange juice and handed it to him. "I feel like I should be making you a well-balanced breakfast and I'm failing you."

"Nah, this is great." Blake sat down, finished the roll, ate another one, and finished his orange juice.

"You want another one?" she asked, tickled at his enthusiastic enjoyment of his meal while wondering if he ever truly felt full.

"No, that's plenty. I'm going to brush my teeth, then I should leave."

Jesse stood looking pensively at the doorway where Blake had just disappeared. "It's really weird, isn't it? Sending him off to school?"

"It is." Something she never thought she'd be able to do. Something she had turned over to

Christina all those years ago. But Christina was gone. And now Blake was here. And she was sharing this moment with Jesse.

Blake popped back into the kitchen and grabbed his backpack. "I'm gonna go now."

Heather jumped up and walked over to him. "Have a good day." She wanted to give him a quick kiss on the forehead. A big hug... or something. Her heart clenched, and she merely gave him an encouraging smile.

"I will." He gave her a quick one-armed hug, and her heart skipped in her chest.

"Bye, Jesse," Blake said as he headed out the door.

The moment the door clicked shut, tears started to flow. Tears. She never cried. Jesse was by her side in two steps. He took her into his arms. "Sh, it's okay." He held her close.

"I know. I just feel like... like this is a miracle. And I'm just so happy." She had just sent her son—who she'd never imagined she'd actually meet—off to school.

"It is a miracle. And I'm glad I got to share it with you."

He continued to hold her in his arms, and that was right where she wanted to be.

~

Heather went to Sea Glass Cafe that afternoon, hoping that Emily would show up and say how Blake's day had gone. Jesse hadn't exactly invited her to come back to his cottage after school, so she didn't want to intrude.

She made herself useful sitting at a table and rolling silverware in napkins for the dinner crowd. She looked up when sunlight spilled in from the door opening and was rewarded to see Emily and Blake enter. Delight spun through her. This was perfect.

She waved to them and they came over to her table, dropping their backpacks. "We came for ice cream. A reward for surviving the first day of school."

"Did you have a good time?" She held her breath, hoping he'd say yes. Hoping it hadn't been too difficult for him to adjust to a new school. Hoping to just hear about his day. Every little tiny detail of it, if she had her way.

He nodded and sat across from her. "I did. Got lost once finding my class, but I'll get it figured out."

"He's got cranky Miss Brady for English, though. That's too bad."

"I'm sure it will be fine," he said.

Emily looked skeptical. "Maybe. Anyway, what flavor ice cream? I'll go get it."

"Vanilla in a cone."

"Heather?"

"Yes, that sounds good. I'll have a vanilla cone, too."

"Be right back. I need to tell Mom I'm here, too." Emily disappeared into the kitchen.

"So it really went okay?" She searched his face.

"It did. Though there's this girl, Jeanie Francis. She hung out by my locker like between every single class. Emily caught me after my last class and showed me the back way out of the school so I could avoid seeing her again."

"I'm sure she'll get the hint soon."

"I'm not sure. But I hope so. She's pretty persistent though."

Emily and Livy returned with their cones. The four of them sat at the table and the kids chattered about their day. She smiled at Livy and her cousin grinned back at her. It was such a normal thing. Hearing about your kid's day at school. And yet she'd never experienced it. It was strange and wonderful at the same time. And it felt so good and so... motherly.

Blake finally stood. "I should go. Going to run by The Destiny and see Jesse, then head home. I can't believe we got so much homework on the first day."

"I'm going to go too. Mom, I'll meet you back at home?" Emily stood and grabbed her backpack.

"I'm working the dinner crowd. I'll be home late."

"Okay, see you whenever. I'm going to knock out my homework, too."

Blake and Emily threaded their way through the tables and disappeared out the door.

"Sounds like Blake had a good day," Livy said.

She turned her attention back to her cousin. "It did sound like that, didn't it? He seemed happy. I hope he's going to fit in and like this school. I know he had a rough time at his last school. I want this to be different."

"It will. And you looked like you were thoroughly enjoying yourself, too."

"I was. It was wonderful to sit here and listen to him talk about his day. All the details. Hearing about his teachers and classmates." She glanced back at the door where he'd disappeared.

"Just like a real mother, right?" Livy grinned.

"Just like." She smiled, beginning to actually feel like a real mother. Like Blake's mother.

CHAPTER 18

Ted stood at the doorway to the balcony of his suite, staring out at the bay, lost in thought. It had been a few weeks since he'd gone with Patricia to Donna's house. He didn't really understand Patricia not wanting to get to know Blake, but he hoped that she'd warm up toward the boy. He seemed like a great kid.

He'd tried to broach the subject with her a few times, but she always shut him down. He wished he could get Patricia to realize what a great thing she had with her big, extended family. But he didn't want to do anything that would make her withdraw from him. They'd come too far.

They went on almost daily walks now down to the harbor. She'd laughed when she told him she'd gone shopping for more practical shoes for their walks. He thought the shoes she'd picked out were still kind of fancy for walking, but at least they didn't have heels.

She had plans with the ladies tonight, and he already missed not having dinner with the group. He'd become a regular at their table in the dining room most evenings. He made a split decision, and before he could talk himself out of it, he picked up his cell phone. As soon as Patricia answered, he drew in a deep breath. "Patricia, how about you come over for dinner tomorrow evening? I'll cook. I'll make chicken piccata for you and we'll have a salad. Dressing on the side?"

"I... well, yes, I could do that."

Not the enthusiastic response that he'd hoped for, but it was still a yes. "Perfect. Six o'clock sound good?"

"I'll be there."

This would be so much better than the full crowd of women that sat with them most nights. He whistled to himself as he headed into the kitchen to make a shopping list. He wanted the dinner to be perfect. They'd have time to talk. Besides, he hadn't had time to cook for her. She was a fairly *particular* eater. He just hoped she liked what he made.

Patricia went to Ted's at six o'clock the next night. More like six-fifteen. She just hadn't been able to decide what to wear. She glanced down at her floral skirt and simple silk blouse, hoping she'd made the right decision and annoyed that it even mattered to her.

Ted answered the door, and she was relieved to see him in nice slacks and shirt. Good, she'd chosen her outfit wisely. Not that she really expected him to be wearing shorts or a t-shirt or something else inappropriate, but it was nice to see he knew how to pick out suitable attire.

"Patricia, come in."

She stepped into his suite. He kept it picked up immaculately. There were no stacks of magazines in disarray, just a hardcover book on the table by the couch. It was a bit masculine for her tastes, but very well done.

"Would you like a drink?"

"I would. How about an old fashioned?"

"I can do that." He went over to the bar and

made them drinks. "We could sit outside unless you think it's too warm. Then we could sit in these chairs by the window. Still have the nice view."

"Inside would be nice." The breeze had picked up, and she'd spent way too much time doing her hair tonight for the breeze to shred her casual, yet elegant, hairdo.

They sat by the window and Ted told her about his day and said that Donna's husband had invited him to go fishing tomorrow. That was interesting. Donna had probably encouraged it. She was always trying to find friends for everyone. A bit interfering as far as Patricia was concerned, but Ted seemed excited to go.

They moved to the breakfast nook when Ted served up dinner. It was too bad these suites didn't have room for a real dining room table, but she supposed the nook area would have to do.

"The meal looks lovely," she said as she sat in the chair Ted held out for her. She appreciated the way he'd plated the meal. It rivaled some of the better presentations in some of her favorite restaurants.

He served a pleasantly cooled white wine with the meal, and the dressing was on the side of the salad as promised. The food was amazingly tasty.

"I didn't know you were such a chef," she complimented him.

"Thank you." Ted beamed at her words. "I do like my cooking. A hobby I took up in my later years."

"You're very good at it. I'm afraid it's something I've never really enjoyed. The cooking, I mean."

He cleared the table, and they sat by the windows again, this time finishing up their glasses of wine.

"This was nice." She looked over at him and smiled. He'd stretched his legs out and a relaxed expression settled on his features. He was such a handsome man. Kind. Funny. A great listener. She remembered all the things she had liked about him so many years ago. He was the same, though a bit more mellow. Of course, he wasn't dealing with running a large hotel now.

"It was very nice. And I'd like to do it again soon."

"I'd like that, too." She was surprised by just how much she'd like that. But she didn't want to overstay her welcome. "I should probably head back to my suite."

He held out a hand to help her to her feet. Not that she needed the help. His firm hands enclosed hers and he pulled her a bit closer than she'd expected. She looked up into his glimmering eyes.

"Ah, Patricia. I've been wanting to kiss you again."

A shock bolted through her at his unexpected remark. He reached out and ran a finger along her cheek, and she shivered slightly, holding her breath.

"Do you think that would be okay with you?"

Before she could give herself a chance to think, she answered him. "Yes, it would." She closed her eyes as his lips pressed gently against hers. Then slowly he pulled away, and the kiss was over.

A bemused look settled on his face. "That was… nice. Like I remembered. Only… better."

"It was nice." Very nice indeed. She hadn't been expecting it, but it was a pleasant surprise. Very pleasant.

He took her hand. "Here, I'll walk you to your suite."

They walked out his door and the few paces down the hallway to hers, holding hands. Her hand felt so right in his yet she was self-conscious of it. So many memories swirled around her. The past with the present.

They stopped at her door, and he grinned at her. "And now I think I'd like another kiss."

Her breath caught and she nodded. He claimed her lips again, this time deepening it slightly, but still ever so gentle. He pulled back and touched her cheek again. "Good night, Patricia."

"Ah… good night." She tried to use her keycard, but it refused to open the door. He took the card from her, swiped it, and she heard the door unlatch. She smiled at him as she slipped inside, closing the door behind her after one last look at him.

She took the few steps needed to reach the couch and sank on the plush cushions, putting her hand up to where he'd touched her cheek. Her heart skittered like a young woman's. Like it had all those years ago.

She wasn't sure what they were doing now. Wasn't sure what she wanted to happen between them. But one thing was certain.

Ted Cabot sure knew how to kiss.

CHAPTER 19

Emily walked into the kitchen and twirled around, her green dress swirling around her. "I'm all ready for the school dance tonight."

Olivia paused from putting the dishes away. "You look lovely, Em. That dress really suits you."

"I found it at the secondhand shop. Isn't it great? And it was five bucks. Such a deal." Emily twirled around again.

"I can't believe it's already the fall dance. Where has the time gone?"

"Ha, easy to say when you aren't the one struggling through chemistry this semester."

A knock came from the front door. "That's probably Blake. We're going to head to the dance together."

"You're walking?"

"Yeah, we decided to. He'll walk me home after, okay?"

"Sure, that's fine." There really were perks to living in a small, safe town. Walkable, so she didn't have to worry about Emily out driving all the time.

Blake came back into the kitchen with Emily.

"You look dashing, Blake."

He flashed a pleased smile. "Dashing, huh?"

"I think that's old people talk for you look great." Emily rolled her eyes, but grinned. "Right, Mom?"

She laughed. "You two go run along. Have a great time."

"We will. It's going to be the greatest dance ever in the history of Moonbeam high school dances. It's so cool that Delbert let us have the pavilion at The Cabot for the dance."

Her daughter was never lacking in enthusiasm. "Have fun. Wake me up when you come home so I can hear all about it."

"Mom, it will still be the same stuff to tell you in the morning." Emily rolled her eyes again and grabbed Blake's elbow. "Come on, let's go. This is going to be spectacular."

She followed them to the front door and watched as they headed down the sidewalk. Who knew that her daughter would find such a great friend in an unexpected cousin?

Ted and Patricia walked out of The Cabot after having a lovely dinner in their dining room. "You want to walk along the harbor a bit? It's cool out this evening," Ted suggested.

"That sounds nice."

He was glad she seemed to be enjoying walking outside more often now. Maybe it was because the beastly heat of the summer was abating. Or maybe she enjoyed his company?

He took her hand in his, and she smiled up at him. He liked that special smile she gave him when they were together. He'd gotten used to having her by his side. And he'd gotten used to kissing her. He couldn't ever get enough of that. She was so refined and proper most of the time, but she was surprisingly passionate with her kisses, which he enjoyed.

They neared the pavilion that was spilling over with teens and a smattering of adults. "I heard the high school is having a dance here tonight. Delbert let them use the pavilion. He's really a great guy, and it seems like he's made quite the success of things. I love seeing The Cabot come alive again. She deserves it."

"The Cabot is very nice." Patricia nodded. "And I'm glad it makes you happy to have it opened up again."

"Let's peek in at the pavilion. I'd love to see the kids having fun."

Patricia looked skeptical about taking in the hubbub but walked with him over to one of the large arched openings to the pavilion. Music floated around them.

It warmed Ted's heart to see the pavilion restored and brimming with people. He paused when he saw Emily standing across the way. He stared at Emily, his brows furrowing. Her hair was pulled up on top of her head and tendrils of red curls framed her face. He frowned. He'd seen that face before. He *knew* that face, that look. Why hadn't he noticed it before tonight?

He slowly turned to look at Patricia, searching her face. "Emily. She looks so much like Cassandra at that age. Like a carbon copy with her hair pulled up. And her smile. That looks like Cassandra's too."

Patricia swiveled, stared across the distance,

and the color ran out of her face. "No, it's just the red hair," she whispered.

He stared at Patricia. "No… I mean, she looks… just… like…" He drew in a sharp breath as his thoughts ping-ponged from the past to the present to Emily. "Like a Cabot."

He should have noticed it before. All the air was sucked away, and he could hardly breathe.

"Patricia?"

She looked away, ignoring him, her shoulders set firmly.

"Patricia, is there something you want to tell me? She's your daughter's granddaughter. Is…" His blood raced through his veins and pounded in his temples as the possibility hammered through him. "Is she my great-granddaughter? Is Donna *my* daughter?"

Patricia slowly turned to face him, her face a mask of protection. "I really don't know. I never wanted to know for certain. I had my suspicions. But… well, Nelson never questioned Donna was his, and you were gone." She shrugged.

Shrugged. Like this wasn't the most explosive thing to happen to him in his whole lifetime. He looked over at Emily again, his heart soaring and his pulse racing. "I have to know, Patricia. I have to."

"*No.* No one is ever going to know for sure. No one. There is no way I want my family to know. I don't want *anyone* to know. It would be... scandalous."

"Patricia, they might be my family. I can't turn my back on that now that I know it might be a possibility." He heard the pleading tone in his voice and didn't care.

She shook her head. "It doesn't matter. They aren't. They can't be."

He looked over at Emily, and certainty flowed through him. "They are my family. I *feel* it. Just look at her."

"Well, we'll never know that for sure, so put your questioning away. Put it away for good."

He turned to her in disbelief. "Are you afraid that Donna and Olivia and Emily will be hurt? Or is it that you don't want people to know what happened that summer?"

"They can't know. No one can know. It was wrong. I was wrong. *We* were wrong. And Donna is Nelson's daughter. That is the end of the discussion."

"Patricia... don't you understand? They might be a part of me. My *family*."

"Ted, we are never going to have this

discussion again. Do you hear me? Never." Her face froze into a hard, determined mask.

"Patricia, I can't just let this drop." The pleading tone was gone, and now his voice held authority and insistence.

Patricia ignored it. "You have to. Now, please take me home. This evening is over."

By the sound of her voice, their newfound friendship was over, too. He took one last long look at Emily, his heart pounding in his chest, and turned to follow Patricia, who was already hurrying away. Away from the truth of their past. Away from the possibility that these women were his family.

Patricia sat in the dark of her suite that night. This was the last thing she'd wanted to come to light. She figured her little secret would be just that. *Her* little secret. And besides, she really didn't know if Nelson or Ted was Donna's father. She'd never wanted to know for sure.

Maybe so she wouldn't feel so guilty…

It was all Nelson's fault, anyway. Him and his not-so-discreet affair that summer. He'd had one the year before but swore it was a onetime thing. Until the next one. Then that summer he'd been totally infatuated with some young blonde woman he'd met. He was rarely home that summer, traveling around the country with this new girl. The town had talked about it some, in whispers at least. She'd been so angry with him. More angry that he wasn't being circumspect than about the fact that he was cheating on her. Again.

And the sideways pitying looks from the town. She couldn't abide by that.

Then suddenly... there was Ted. Understanding. Friendly. Easy to talk to. He didn't criticize her every move. He complimented her. Told her she looked lovely. She'd been swept away with their friendship.

Until one night, their friendship had deepened, and she'd slept with him. Not actually as revenge against Nelson's infidelities, but partly for that reason. But mostly because she'd begun to have feelings for Ted. She'd held this tiny hope in her heart that maybe someday they could be together. That she could someday have a relationship with someone who cared about her and respected her.

Even though Nelson constantly cheated on her, she'd still felt guilty about the handful of times she slept with Ted. She hated the sneaking around feeling. But those times in his arms, those she'd treasured.

And she'd never had another affair with anyone. Ever.

But she had slept with Ted, and then he disappeared. She was devastated. After he was gone, she began to suspect she was pregnant. And there was still every probability that her child was Nelson's. A small probability, but it was there.

So she'd ignored the doubt. Ignored it for all these years. Even when Olivia had her red-haired, green-eyed daughter. She'd convinced herself that was just a coincidence.

But none of this mattered. It all had to be kept in the past. She'd made that perfectly clear to Ted. Insisted. And he'd have to listen to her. He had to. There was no way the secret could come out.

CHAPTER 20

"Ted's been in here almost every day this week, I think," Donna said to Evelyn as he came walking into the store yet again.

"He's been eating at the cafe most days, too. Though Mother hasn't been with him even once. Not that our cafe food is to her liking. But I kind of thought the two of them were a thing these days."

"Do you serve salad with dressing on the side? If not, she won't be coming here." Donna grinned at her sister.

"Hi, Ted. What brings you in today?" Donna asked as Ted came walking up to her.

"I need an extension cord. Moving some things around in my suite at Sunrise."

He had on his usual friendly smile, but he

seemed to be searching, a bit uneasy. There was this look of sadness tinged with hope in his eyes. But why would that be? She was probably imagining it.

"We've got them. Here, I'll show you. I'll catch you in a bit, Evelyn." She led Ted over to the electrical area. "All lengths. Indoor. Outdoor. Take your pick."

Ted picked out a six-foot indoor cord and turned to her. "Your store is really nice. Well supplied and organized. I really like that it looks like an old-fashioned general store."

"Thanks, Ted."

"Do you... do you like working here?"

Curious question. "Yes, I do. I love it here. Took over running it when my grandparents retired."

"I don't suppose Patricia had any interest in running the store."

Donna laughed. "Not at all. Besides, she was always traveling with my father. Well, most of the time. Or doing business parties or events at the country club. She had no interest in the store. But I love it. There's so much history here." She flung her arm out. "I'm surrounded by it."

Ted seemed genuinely interested in her

answers. "So if I remember my Moonbeam history correctly, a Grace Parker started the store with her husband. In the 1920s, I believe."

She was surprised he knew that much, but then he had grown up in Moonbeam when his family had owned the hotel. "Yes, she was my great-grandmother. Then my grandmother, Mary Lou McFarland, ran it with my grandfather. I grew up helping out in the store and took on more responsibility as I got older. When they decided to retire, they gave me the store to run."

"And your daughter, Livy, runs the cafe?"

"She does. Opening the cafe was all her idea, and she's made quite the success of it. Of course, it doesn't hurt that we have Evelyn as the cook. She's a wonderful chef."

"I can attest to that." He nodded. "I've been in there quite a few times."

Like every day this week, if what Evelyn had told her was correct.

"And her daughter, Emily, works there, too?"

"She does. Along with working at the history museum—she's way into history—and she does the social media for the general store and the cafe."

"She sounds very busy."

"She is. And she's smart and works hard at school. She's hoping for a scholarship to college."

"Sounds like a wonderful young lady."

"She is." She glanced over to see more customers coming in. "So, did you need anything else?"

"Ah, no. This is all." They headed back to the checkout. She rang him out and handed him his purchase. "See you soon."

He stared at her for a long moment, then smiled. "Yes, I'm sure I'll be back soon."

He walked out the door, and she frowned. Maybe he was lonely and came in here for some company? Maybe things between her mother and Ted hadn't worked out. She wasn't certain.

But one thing was certain. Ted Cabot sure liked coming to Parker's.

CHAPTER 21

Ted knew Patricia was avoiding him. She had been for the last week or so. She no longer joined the group at dinner. She didn't answer his calls. And she'd made it perfectly clear that he would never know if Donna, Livy, and Emily were his family.

Which was unacceptable. He didn't want to upset anyone's life, but he had to know. Had to.

But if he could never talk to Patricia, he didn't know how that was going to happen. He didn't want to be the person to tell Donna. Patricia should. But she'd made it abundantly clear that the secret would never come out. Even if he felt in his soul that Emily was a Cabot. It was so clear to him. How did other people not see it?

He'd started going to Parker's every day with one excuse or another. Eating at the cafe and watching as Livy served the customers. Stopping by the shop and letting Donna help him find whatever item he thought was reasonable that he might be shopping for. He'd even had ice cream at the counter with Emily one day after school, and he could hardly stop staring at her and her curly red hair and flashing green eyes. The Cabot green eyes. She was truly a mirror image of Cassandra at that age. Especially when she pulled her hair up.

He looked around his suite in frustration and decided to go for a walk. He laughed, wondering if he'd end up at Parker's yet again. He hadn't been since his extension cord expedition yesterday.

He went downstairs and out the open doorway to the wide deck that stretched across the back of the main building. The deck was empty except for one lone figure sitting on a chair at the end of the deck.

Patricia.

Perfect timing.

He strode down the wooden planks and stood in front of her. "I've been trying to reach you."

She looked up at him. "There's really nothing we have to say." She jumped out of her chair and started walking away from him.

"We have to talk. I want to know. I deserve to know." He hurried to keep pace with her and gently caught her arm.

She whirled around near the doorway and squared off with him. "No. No one can ever know. I've told you that. There is nothing to discuss."

He stood with his back to the doorway and blocked her way inside. "No, we do have to talk."

"Sh. Lower your voice. And I've got nothing to say." Her eyes flashed in defiance.

"But Donna might be my daughter." His temper rose along with the volume of his voice.

Suddenly the color drained from Patricia's face, and she gasped, staring over his shoulder. He turned around to see what had caught her attention.

Donna stood there, her eyes wide and an incredulous look etched on her face. Like a child who'd just been told Santa Claus wasn't real and her world as she knew it had exploded.

~

Donna reached to grab hold of the doorframe and stared at her mother and then at Ted. *What had she just heard?*

"Mother?" She couldn't possibly have heard what she was certain she *had* heard.

"Donna, what are you doing here?" Her mother stood there, her back straight and ignoring her question.

"I wasn't eavesdropping. Evelyn and I were just coming to see if you wanted to come over for brunch on Sunday. We haven't seen you in a while. Evelyn stopped off to chat with the concierge. Eugene. Nice man. I'm sure she'll be along in a minute." Why was she rambling about details? "Anyway, I came out here, and I heard…" She turned to Ted. "I heard you say that I might be your daughter? I did hear that correctly, didn't I?"

Ted nodded, and her mother threw him a murderous glare.

"But how?"

Her mother shook her head at Ted, commanding his silence without a word.

She rushed on. "I mean, I know *how* it could happen. The mechanics. But… Mother?"

"Sh, Donna. Lower your voice."

"That's what you want to say to me now? Lower my voice?"

"We don't want people to hear you." Patricia frowned and glanced around.

"You don't want people to hear me?" Her voice got louder. "Hear me? Do *you* hear me? Are you going to answer my question?"

She sensed more than saw someone come up to her side and felt her sister's arm encircle her waist.

"What's going on?" Evelyn asked.

She glanced at Evelyn. "Ted here just asked Mother if I was his daughter."

Evelyn gasped. "What?"

"Right. But Mother hasn't given me an answer."

"Maybe we should go somewhere quieter where we can be alone," Ted said, staring at her as if memorizing every detail about her.

That was okay because she was staring back at him looking for any common features. Did she have his chin?

"No, we can talk here. Now," Donna insisted. "I want to know the truth."

"Ted is confused. That's all." Her mother shook her head, but a hint of fear clouded her eyes.

"Why would he think that I'm his daughter?"

Ted looked at her mother. "I'm sorry, Patricia." He cleared his throat and turned back to her. "I saw… I saw Emily at the dance. She looked just like Cassandra did at that age. The red hair. There's even something about her smile. And her green eyes."

Donna stared at Ted. Her sister was staring at him, too. Those green eyes of his. So like Emily's.

"It's a Cabot thing. I have them. Cassandra has them. My grandfather had them."

"But…" She looked from Ted—and his green eyes—back to her mother.

Her mother looked away.

"Tell me. Did you sleep with Ted? It would have to have been when you were married to Father."

Her mother looked back at her but didn't answer.

"You did, didn't you? I mean, I know that Father cheated on you. It was so obvious once I was old enough to know what was going on. But I never thought that you…" Not that she really was judging her mother here. Her father had treated her horribly and had affair after affair.

She never understood why her mother stayed with him.

But this thing with Ted. *That* surprised her.

And she deserved to know the truth.

"Mother, please answer me."

Patricia drew herself up to her full height and in all the haughtiness that she was known for, she looked at Donna. "I really don't know who your father is. Which one. Nelson or Ted. I just… never knew."

"But—"

"And there is no reason to know now. No reason for needless gossip. Nelson considered you his daughter. Never questioned it. So there is no reason to find out the truth after all this time."

"Oh, yes there is, Mother. There is. Because if Ted is my father… I want to know." She turned to Ted. "Don't you?"

"I do. I really want to know." He reached out and took her hand. "Looking at Emily, I'm already ninety-five percent certain."

She stood there clinging to his hand while the whole world she knew spun out of control around her.

"Evie?" She looked over at her sister, hoping for support, for… something.

"It's going to be okay, Donna. It won't change who you are." Evie's eyes shone with the sisterly support she so desperately needed.

Only… maybe her half-sister? Her world began spinning yet again.

She looked back at Ted—the man who might be her father. "So we'll get tested to find out?"

"Yes. As soon as possible." He squeezed her hand.

And suddenly, she wanted it to be true. Wanted this kind, wonderful man as her father. The test would tell her the truth.

But she needed to go clear her head. Needed… She wasn't sure what she needed other than to get away from her mother.

"I… I think I'm going to go for a walk. I need some time alone."

"I'll go with you," Evie said.

"No, I really want to be alone. Will you give Ted my phone number? And Ted, on Monday I'll meet you at the clinic in town and we'll have tests run?"

"I'd appreciate that. Yes. I'll meet you."

She gave one last long look at her mother and turned and headed down to the harbor walk. Thoughts swirled around in her mind and tears began to roll down her cheeks. She might not even be who she always thought she was. It was so much to take in.

Her mother was always about proper. Make sure there was no scandal. No gossip. Yet she'd had an *affair*. Donna simply could not reconcile the mother she knew with a woman who would have an affair.

About twenty minutes into her walk, Barry jogged up to her. "Hey." He opened his arms, and she walked into his embrace. "Evelyn called me and told me what happened. It's going to be okay." He stroked her hair, holding her close.

"Everything I thought I knew is just… gone."

"I'm not gone. You know I love you. I always will love you. Whether Nelson or Ted is your father. It doesn't matter to me." He kissed her forehead. "I know it matters to you, though. You want to know the truth."

She pressed her cheek against his chest, drinking in his strength, letting his embrace slowly stop the whirling world around her. Monday. She and Ted would get their tests run on Monday. Then they'd just have to wait for the results.

CHAPTER 22

T ed met Donna at the clinic on Monday, more nervous than he ever remembered being. "You doing okay?" he asked her as she sat beside him in the waiting room.

"I'm not really sure. My world is just... I mean, nothing will be the same."

His heart squeezed in his chest. As happy as he'd be to know he had all this family, he hated to see the upset Donna was going through.

"I wanted to call and tell Cassandra, but decided to wait until the official results of the tests came back."

"I haven't said anything to Olivia or Emily either. I just... well, we'll see what the results say."

The nice technician took care of them and

explained they'd both get emails where they could click on a link and use a code to get their results. It would take a few days. He wasn't sure how he'd make it through the hours until he knew for certain.

They walked out of the clinic and into the sunshine. He turned to Donna. "Would you like to get a bite to eat?"

"You know. I would. Can we go somewhere besides the cafe? How about Jimmy's out on the wharf?"

"I've never been there. Anywhere you'd like is great with me. Shall I drive us over?"

"Can we walk? I need... some air."

"Walking is always fine with me." They headed down the sidewalk. He couldn't get the idea out of his mind that he might be walking down the sidewalk with his *daughter*.

"This is strange, isn't it? Walking together." Donna paused and shoved her hair away from her face.

"I was just thinking the same thing."

"I don't know how I'm going to make it until we hear."

He laughed. "And I just thought that, too."

"How about I introduce you to the coldest,

best craft beer in Moonbeam and the best fish tacos, too? That might get our minds off of it."

They sat at tables by the railing at Jimmy's and Donna was right. The cold beer was perfect, and the tacos didn't disappoint.

"So, tell me about yourself. I mean, if you want to." He looked across the table at this woman who might be his daughter.

Probably. Maybe.

The words taunted him.

"Well, I grew up here in Moonbeam. My grandmother mostly raised Evelyn and me. Mother and Father—and, uh, *Nelson*—traveled a lot for business. They'd go to Europe for months at a time. But it was great. I adored my grandmother."

"And Olivia's father?"

"Ah, yes. Charlie Brian Foster. I'd say he was a mistake, but then I got Olivia from marrying him. He's been mostly out of our lives for years. Rarely see him."

"I'm sorry."

"It was just one of those things. He wasn't cut out to be a father... or a husband."

"But you found Barry. You two seem very happy." He loved seeing the way Barry's eyes lit up when he looked at Donna. She deserved a man who loved her like that.

"We are happy. Very. I was lucky to find him."

"And tell me about Olivia and Emily."

"Olivia got pregnant in college and moved home. Emily's father—Brett—they never married. He wasn't much of a father either. He does see Emily occasionally. He even took her to Paris, but… well, that didn't work out well. Olivia is engaged to Austin now, and that's what matters. He's a wonderful man. I'm so pleased."

"Okay, I know I'm asking a hundred questions. But Emily?"

"Ah, our Emily. She's one of a kind. Full of boundless energy. Smart as a whip. Generous and kind. She's… wonderful."

"Sounds like you have many blessings in your life."

"That I do. And I'm grateful for every one of them."

He wondered if she'd be grateful for him. If she'd consider him a blessing in her life, or just the man who upended the world she knew and all she knew about herself.

Donna stood in the kitchen of the cafe and checked her phone for the millionth time since she and Ted had the paternity test at the clinic. It had been two days, and she was about at the end of her rope with waiting.

"You okay?" Evelyn came up behind her.

"I just want to know for sure."

"Mother still won't talk to you?"

"No. She won't answer her phone. I'm so angry right now that it's probably for the best. But I will talk to her. When I find out the truth. Whatever the truth is." She turned to Evie. "And you know, I might only be your half-sister. That's so strange to think about."

Evelyn hugged her tightly. "You aren't half anything to me. We grew up together. You're my best friend. Nothing changes that. Nothing."

"You're the best sister ever, Evie." She put her phone back in her pocket. "Come on, since Melody is off today, I'll peel peaches while you make pie crust. It will give me something to do besides pulling my phone out every other minute."

They made the pies, then Evelyn made both of them some tea. "Sit. I could use a break before worrying about the dinner crowd."

She sat across from Evelyn, mindlessly

dunking the teabag in the steaming water. She looked up to see Ted standing in the doorway. "The girl at the checkout at Parker's told me you were here."

"You found me."

Ted's eyes were glistening, and he had the widest possible smile, one that looked like he'd gotten Christmas, his first snowfall, and an impossible wish granted, all wrapped up in one.

She jumped up and grabbed her phone and saw she had an email. She looked at Ted. "You got the results."

"I did." He crossed over and took her hands in his. "And... I'm your father." Tears filled the corners of his eyes.

"Oh." She stood there in stunned silence for a few moments until a grin began to spread across her lips. "That is... wonderful." And she threw herself into her father's arms for the first time in her life. A sense of rightness flowed through her. A sense of parental acceptance and belonging like she'd never experienced before this moment.

He finally released her and stepped back. "And now I have a family. Lots of family."

"You know we Parker women come as a package deal, right?" Donna grinned at him.

"Along with me and Olivia and Emily, there's Evelyn, too. And Heather. And all the guys. You just might have gotten more than you bargained for."

"I just might have gotten more than I'd ever hoped." Ted's eyes still glistened and the purest look of happiness she'd ever seen settled on his features. Her father's face. Her *father*.

CHAPTER 23

Patricia had seen Ted out the window, walking along the harbor, so she knew it was safe to answer the door when she heard a knock. Maybe it was Betsy coming to check on her yet again. The woman just could not take a hint that she wanted to be left alone. And what would Betsy think if she knew the truth, anyway? Not that she'd ever find out.

She opened the door and frowned.

"What are you doing here, Donna?

"I came to tell you the results." Her daughter breezed past her without even bothering to wait for an invite. She'd raised her better than that.

She closed the door and turned to see her daughter standing with her arms crossed. She held her breath, knowing that she'd finally know the truth. Though she was fairly certain what Donna was going to say. She'd felt in her bones that Ted was Donna's father since the moment she'd held her.

"Ted's my father. But you knew that, didn't you?"

"I thought probably." She nodded. "Now that you know, you can't tell anyone.

"Ah, but yes, I can. And I will. I will tell Olivia and Emily. And I want everyone to know. He's a wonderful man and I couldn't ask for a better father. You know, Father was—*Nelson was* —he was cold and critical, and I never could please him. Ever. That's not how a father should be."

"Nelson was…" Her mother shrugged. "Nelson. He did the best he could."

"No, he didn't. He didn't try. Not with Evelyn and not with me." She paused and looked at her mother and couldn't help the sympathy that flowed through her, even as angry as she was right now. "And he didn't try with you."

"But we can't have the town talking about this. Everyone will know that… that I had an affair. I can't bear for people to know."

"Mother, you're going to have to toughen up. Accept it. It's a consequence of your actions. We all have to deal with the consequences of our choices, even you. You need to deal with Ted being my father, and you need to deal with Blake being Heather's son. If you can, then you're welcome at our family brunch this Sunday. But if you can't... then I'd rather you not come."

Donna spun around and headed to the door. She paused, one hand on the doorknob. "But I really hope you can accept all this. I really do." And with that, her daughter slipped out the door, leaving her alone.

All alone.

And maybe living out the rest of her days alone if she couldn't come to grips with the fact that Ted Cabot was Donna's father and soon all of Moonbeam would know that fact.

CHAPTER 24

That evening Donna insisted Olivia and Emily come by for dessert out on the point. She'd asked Ted to come, too, and she was going to tell them the truth. Strangely, she wasn't nervous about it. She just wanted everyone to know. But her daughter and granddaughter first. Well, she'd told Barry, of course. And she was glad to have him with her when she told the girls.

Ted showed up early, laughing. "Sorry, I got impatient."

"Come outside with me and have a beer while Donna fusses in the kitchen," Barry said. "The girls will be here soon." Barry grabbed two beers from the fridge, and the men headed outside.

She cut some pieces of the chocolate cake she'd brought home from the cafe. She could always depend on Evelyn to make the perfect dessert. She peered outside and saw that Olivia and Emily had come in the back way and stood out there with Barry and Ted.

Ted, who was staring at both of them with a silly grin on his face. It made her smile just watching him. Her father. He'd be a fabulous grandfather and great-grandfather. As soon as she broke the news.

She headed out with a tray of iced tea and cake. Emily started to reach for a piece of cake. "Evelyn's, right? She's the best."

"I first wanted to talk to you and Olivia." Donna set down the tray.

Olivia and Emily looked at her questioningly. "Mom, is everything okay?" A worried look crossed Olivia's face.

"I have some news. It affects both of you. Good news. Don't worry." She glanced over at Ted and saw him nervously run his hands down the side of his slacks. She took in a deep breath. "I found out something. Something I'm happy about. I hope you will be, too. You see—" She held out her hand for Ted, and he came over and took it in his. "I found out that Ted is my father."

Olivia's and Emily's mouths dropped open.

"And I'm very happy about it, too," Ted added, his voice shaking the tiniest bit. "Hopefully you can be, too. I know it changes what you've known about your family."

"But now Ted is our family, too." She waited for the girls to say something.

"So, Grandmother had…" Olivia started, then paused, her eyes full of disbelief.

"An affair. Yes. It's a long story. And I'm not judging her. I hope you won't either."

"And Ted… he's your father?" Emily's brows lifted. "Wow. Great-grandfather—oh, I guess he's not now—*Nelson* never liked me, anyway. So I'm cool with this."

"I, for one, can't wait to get to know you."

Olivia broke into a smile and approached Ted. "Welcome to the family." She threw her arms around him and gave him a hug. Emily hurried over and did the same.

Tears pricked the corners of Donna's eyes at the sight of the three of them holding each other. Ted held out an arm, and she joined their group hug.

A family.

They finally all stepped back, and it was clear that Ted was fighting back tears. "I'm so incredibly happy. So blessed. I never thought I'd have a child, much less a whole family."

"Just remember you said that," Emily teased. "We're kind of a handful, you know."

Ted didn't look worried. He looked extremely happy. She glanced over at Barry and he sent her a warm, delighted smile.

Things were different now, but in so many ways, still the same. A feeling of peace swept through her as she watched Olivia, Emily, and Ted talking and laughing. Emily asked Ted about a million questions, and he good-naturedly answered each one.

Barry walked over and took her hand in his, squeezing it tightly. Family was a mercurial thing. It could change with a wedding, or a death, or... by finding out who you really were.

Ted went over to Patricia's suite the next day and knocked on her door. She didn't answer, of course. He knocked again.

"I know you're in there," he called. "I'm not leaving until you open the door."

Still no answer.

"Patricia. Open up." He spoke even louder, knowing that if he was loud enough, she'd have to open the door because she wouldn't want other people in the hallway to hear him. "We need to talk."

He finally heard stirrings inside and the lock clicking open. She opened the door a tiny sliver. "Go away. And be quiet. People will hear you."

"No, we need to talk. Let me in." He didn't lower his voice at all.

She stared at him for a few moments, then stepped away from the door. He entered her suite and closed the door behind him.

"I don't know what you want to talk about. I asked you not to do this. Not to… change everything."

"I had to know. Donna wanted to know. And we told Olivia and Emily last night."

"You didn't."

"Of course, we did. They're my family now, too. And I couldn't be more pleased."

Patricia shook her head and stepped away from him. "This is all wrong. But probably what I deserve for having an affair with you. That was wrong. This is wrong." She shook her head.

"I admit. The affair was wrong. It was. You

were married, even if Nelson was cheating on you all the time. That didn't make it right. And I was married, even though Bianca had said she was divorcing me." He walked over closer to her. "But I'm glad it happened. I'm glad we had Donna. You've given me something that I never dreamed I'd have. A daughter. And Olivia and Emily. I'm so incredibly happy."

"The whole town will be talking."

"Probably. For a while. Then they'll find something else to talk about and soon it will just be a fact of life, not some big news."

"It was supposed to be my secret. No one would ever know." Real pain was etched across her face and a haunted look clung to her eyes.

His heart ached for her pain. It was clear she was struggling and there was nothing he could do for her. He reached out and took her hands. "Sometimes secrets have a way of coming out into the open like this one. I know it will be hard for you. I know that. And I'm sorry you'll have to go through that."

"I don't think I can." She shook her head.

"You're stronger than you think. And I think you should come to Donna's brunch on Sunday. She said she asked you… but only if you're okay with all of this. Come to brunch with me. I'll be there with you. For you. I promise it will all be fine. You just need to accept the truth and find a way to make peace with it."

"I'm not sure I can." She stared down at their hands.

"Only you can make that decision, Patricia. But I have every faith in you. I always have. You're a remarkable woman. You'll find a way to make peace. And we'll both enjoy our family." He paused, then plunged on, knowing he might be pushing his luck. "Also… I'd still like to… to date you. To get back to being friends again. I've missed you."

He slowly searched her face, but it gave him no answer. He let go of her hands and started for the door. "I'll knock on your door at noon on Sunday. If you answer, we'll go to brunch together. We'll start over. Try again. If you don't answer… well, I'll know your decision and I'll go alone."

CHAPTER 25

On Sunday morning, Cassandra Cabot watched out of the plane's window as they circled the airport and came in for a landing. She couldn't keep the silly grin off her face. She had family now! More than Uncle Ted. There was Donna, and Livy, and Emily. She never thought she'd have this. And yet her uncle had given her the best surprise when he'd called to tell her.

Then Donna had called her and said they were having a big family brunch and asked her to come. So she'd arranged her schedule so she could fly in and surprise Ted. Delbert had enthusiastically agreed to pick her up at the airport. She had to admit she was as excited to see him as she was to see her new family.

The plane landed, and she waited her turn, then grabbed her overnight bag from above. She walked down the gangway and into the terminal, glancing for the signs to baggage claim where Delbert said he'd meet her.

She found her way, but there was no sign of him yet. She spotted the right carousel and searched for her suitcase among the luggage drifting around and around.

"There you are." Delbert walked up to her and gave her a smile that made her heart skip. She'd missed him. More than she thought she would.

He wrapped her in a hug and held her a little bit longer than necessary. Which suited her just fine. She finally spotted her bag and Delbert swung it off the carousel.

"I can't wait to get to Donna's. It's just such unexpected news."

"It sure is. Ted's been over to The Cabot and told me. So I wasn't too surprised when you called and said you were coming to Moonbeam." He adjusted the suitcase to pull along with them. "And I was pretty pleased to hear you were coming back to town, too."

"I can't stay long. Just a few days."

Disappointment swept across his features,

but he quickly hid it. "Well, then we'll have to make the most of those days, won't we?"

"We shall." She smiled at him. She couldn't wait to be back in Moonbeam. And see her uncle. And see all these new family members. People she knew but had no idea were her relatives before this.

Delbert took her hand in his and she glanced down at it. Okay, and she was pleased to be back to see Delbert again, too.

Right before noon, Donna nervously set out mimosas and tea. Beer sat chilling in a bucket of ice.

Evelyn walked over and set down a tray of sandwiches. "It's going to be fine. Our first big family gathering."

"I don't know why I'm nervous. Do you think Mother will come?" She glanced inside where Barry was talking to Olivia and Emily.

"I honestly don't know. She hates scandal and gossip and is always insisting we have to have certain standards in our family. Now she has to face the fact that *she's* the center of the gossip. She'll hate that. I'm not sure if she'll ever come out of her suite at this point."

"I told her she was welcome if she can accept all this. That everyone will know that Ted is my father. I'm *thrilled* to have him as my father."

Evelyn shrugged. "I'm just not sure. You know how Mother is."

"I know, I know. You always tell me to not get my hopes up. Not to expect Mother to change at this stage of her life. You're probably right." She gave Evelyn a small smile. "Heck, you're always right."

"I hate to see you hurt by her. But you'll be okay. Even if she never accepts that Ted is your father."

"No sign of Grandmother," Olivia said as she and Heather came out to the lanai.

"She's probably not coming." Donna was strangely hurt. Like her mother was rejecting her. Which was silly, but it was how she felt.

She turned to see Barry leading Cassandra and Delbert outside.

"Look who's here," Barry said.

They walked over and Cassandra gave her a big hug. "Thank you for inviting me. I was so happy after Uncle Ted told me the news and couldn't wait to see all of you again. I wouldn't miss this first big family get-together for anything. Wow, we're *family*." Her face was filled with the same awe that Donna felt when she found out. "Oh, and I hope you don't mind that Delbert's here. I asked him to pick me up at the airport so I could surprise Uncle Ted."

"We're glad to have both of you."

"You sure I'm not barging in on a family thing?" Delbert stood close to Cassandra's side.

"No, the more the merrier," she assured him.

"Gosh, I have more family now. I'm just… thrilled. It's only been Ted and me for years." Cassandra took Delbert's arm and Donna hid a smile. Yes, she was sure something was going on between those two. Only time would tell.

"Well, now you have all of this." She flung her hand wide. All of this, but not Patricia. Her mother was never going to accept this big, blended family.

"Hey." Evelyn came up to her and tilted her head toward the doorway to the lanai.

Donna turned and looked that direction. There in the doorway stood her mother with Ted at her side, firmly holding her hand.

She looked… scared? Was that the look on

her face? Donna had never seen her mother look frightened of anything. Ever. Her mother didn't get scared. She just frowned away her problems.

But not this one.

A tentative sliver of hope crept through her as she swooped up a mimosa and headed over to her mother. "Hello, Mother. Would you like a mimosa?"

"I'd love one." Her voice shook slightly, and so did her hand as she reached for the drink.

"I'm glad you came."

"Thank you for inviting me," she said formally.

"Ted, hi." She greeted him. Her father. She was still having a hard time getting used to that.

He beamed at her, but still kept his hand locked with her mother's. Then he saw Cassandra and broke into an even bigger smile. "Cassie, you're here. What a great surprise."

"You didn't think I was going to miss the first big family get-together, did you?" Cassandra hurried over and hugged him.

Ted hugged her back with one arm but still held her mother's hand.

"Ted, why don't you go over and grab yourself a beer. And Cassandra, there are mimosas over there too. Join the family." Donna pointed toward the drinks.

"Perfect." Cassandra headed over to the drinks with Delbert right at her side.

Ted turned to her mother. "Shall we?"

"Wait." Her mother stopped him.

Donna held her breath, dreading what words might come next.

Her mother looked around. "I was wondering where Blake was... I'd like to sit down and talk to him and get to know him."

Donna's mouth gaped open in surprise. She recovered—slightly—and called out, "Emily, bring Blake out here, will you?"

"Thank you," her mother said. "I appreciate it. And I appreciate the invitation to brunch. This is nice."

Her mother had actually thanked her. And a compliment. Well, there was a first time for everything.

Blake and Emily came outside and her mother turned to them. "Would you two like to join me over there at the table in the shade? Tell me about how school is going."

Emily's eyes widened in surprise. Of course they did. Patricia knew she'd never taken this much interest in Emily's life. But that was changing now. She couldn't make up for how she'd acted before, but she was responsible for how she acted in the future.

Ted gave her an encouraging look and squeezed her hand before she went and joined the kids.

She settled into her chair uncertain how to even start a conversation with Emily and Blake. She hadn't had any deep conversations with her girls when they were young. Or now, for that matter. This out of control feeling didn't suit her one bit, but she cleared her throat, determined to make this work. "So, you two go to Moonbeam High School?" Of course they did, but she was searching for how to start, what to say.

Emily and Blake nodded.

"Do you like school?" She was still struggling.

"I do. And I'm trying to get a scholarship to help pay for college," Emily said.

"I like the school, too. Emily's introduced me to tons of kids," Blake added.

And now it was time to tackle the whole

Heather and Jesse and Blake predicament. "And I hear that Jesse has started legal proceedings so you can live with him permanently." She was well aware that she'd treated Heather and Blake horribly when she'd heard about Heather having a baby with Jesse and keeping that a secret from everyone. Even Jesse. How was that different than her keeping a secret about Donna? Even though she had always tried to convince herself that Donna might be Nelson's. She'd known in her heart that Donna was Ted's daughter. She just hadn't admitted it.

"He is. I'm really excited about it but it's taking forever."

"Blake, I'm sorry that it took me a bit of time to get used to having you in our family." She reached across the table and covered his hand. "But I'm really happy to have you in our family and hope to get to know you better."

Emily's eyes widened again and her mouth dropped open, then she struggled to cover her surprise by taking a large swallow of her soda.

She caught herself just in time before correcting Emily to take smaller sips of her drink.

"I'd like to get to know you better, too." Blake smiled and seemed to relax.

This wasn't so hard. She could learn to do this. Get to know not only Emily and Blake, but Donna, Evelyn, Olivia, and Heather, too. It just might take some time. She could change. She *would*.

She glanced across the lanai and Ted smiled at her. She smiled back at him. So much had changed since she and Ted had moved back to Moonbeam. Changed for the better. Maybe, with more time, she could finally feel like she belonged.

Donna made her rounds, making sure everyone had drinks, and she reveled in the sounds of laughter. It was such a perfect day filled with family.

Evelyn slipped up beside her and whispered in her ear. "What do you think is going on with Delbert and Cassandra? He hasn't taken his eyes off her since they got here."

"I'm not sure, but I think something is going on between them. Hope so. I'm for everyone being happy." She grinned as happiness bubbled through her.

"And what do you think will happen with

Ted and Mother now?" Evelyn glanced over at Ted who kept glancing at their mother, a pleased, self-satisfied smile on his face.

"I have no clue." But hey, she wanted her mother and Ted to be happy too. She wanted the whole *world* to be as happy as she was right now. "But I'm proud of her for coming to brunch. This was quite the Parker family secret, wasn't it?"

"It was." Evelyn laughed. "And I know I said to quit expecting Mother to change, but I was wrong. So very wrong. Look at her."

She glanced over at her mother chatting with Emily and Blake. Her mother actually looked like she was enjoying the conversation.

She turned back to her sister and grinned. "Never underestimate the strength of a Parker woman."

Dear Reader,

I hope you enjoyed The Parker Family Secret. Next up is book five, Grace Parker's Peach Pie. This is Evelyn's story.

And I can't wait for you to read book six, The Perks of Being a Parker. Just wait until you see what Camille is up to! Will this finally be the last of her?

As always, thanks for reading my books. I truly appreciate each and every one of you!

Kay

AFTERWARD - NEXT IN SERIES

Are you ready for the next book in the series?

Grace Parker's Peach Pie, Book 5

Evelyn is thankful that Parker Cafe—oops, Sea Glass Cafe—is finally profitable and growing. The townsfolk love to come in for the sweet, mouthwatering delights she bakes... especially the old family recipe for peach pie.

Is it the peach pie that keeps bringing Rob Bentley back to the cafe, day after day?

Rob is in Moonbeam helping his sister, Violet, restore the very neglected Murphy's Resort. A resort she bought without consulting him and he thinks is a terrible idea. But when had Violet ever listened to his advice?

Heather and Jesse can't catch a break either. Their son gets into serious trouble at school. Trouble he swears he wasn't involved in, but all the evidence points toward him.

Read more about the lives of the Parker women. More secrets are revealed. And yet another town festival as Evelyn and Rob become friends... and maybe a bit more. Oh, and a wedding. But who's getting married?

Grace Parker's Peach Pie is book five in the Moonbeam Bay series.

MOONBEAM BAY - the series

ALSO BY KAY CORRELL

COMFORT CROSSING ~ THE SERIES

The Shop on Main - Book One

The Memory Box - Book Two

The Christmas Cottage - A Holiday Novella (Book 2.5)

The Letter - Book Three

The Christmas Scarf - A Holiday Novella (Book 3.5)

The Magnolia Cafe - Book Four

The Unexpected Wedding - Book Five

The Wedding in the Grove (crossover short story between series - Josephine and Paul from The Letter.)

LIGHTHOUSE POINT ~ THE SERIES

Wish Upon a Shell - Book One

Wedding on the Beach - Book Two

Love at the Lighthouse - Book Three

Cottage near the Point - Book Four

Return to the Island - Book Five

Bungalow by the Bay - Book Six

CHARMING INN ~ Return to Lighthouse Point

One Simple Wish - Book One

Two of a Kind - Book Two

Three Little Things - Book Three

Four Short Weeks - Book Four

Five Years or So - Book Five

Six Hours Away - Book Six

Charming Christmas - Book Seven

SWEET RIVER ~ THE SERIES

A Dream to Believe in - Book One

A Memory to Cherish - Book Two

A Song to Remember - Book Three

A Time to Forgive - Book Four

A Summer of Secrets - Book Five

A Moment in the Moonlight - Book Six

MOONBEAM BAY ~ THE SERIES

The Parker Women - Book One

The Parker Cafe - Book Two

A Heather Parker Original - Book Three

The Parker Family Secret - Book Four

Grace Parker's Peach Pie - Book Five

The Perks of Being a Parker - Book Six

INDIGO BAY ~ Save by getting Kay's complete collection of stories previously published separately in the multi-author Indigo Bay series. The three stories are all interconnected.

Sweet Days by the Bay

Or buy them separately:

Sweet Sunrise - Book Three

Sweet Holiday Memories - A short holiday story

Sweet Starlight - Book Nine

ABOUT THE AUTHOR

Kay writes sweet, heartwarming stories that are a cross between women's fiction and contemporary romance. She is known for her charming small towns, quirky townsfolk, and enduring strong friendships between the women in her books.

Kay lives in the Midwest of the U.S. and can often be found out and about with her camera, taking a myriad of photographs which she likes to incorporate into her book covers. When not lost in her writing or photography, she can be found spending time with her ever-supportive husband, knitting, or playing with her puppies —two cavaliers and one naughty but adorable Australian shepherd. Kay and her husband also love to travel. When it comes to vacation time, she is torn between a nice trip to the beach or the mountains—but the mountains only get considered in the summer—she swears she's allergic to snow.

Learn more about Kay and her books at
kaycorrell.com

While you're there, sign up for her newsletter to
hear about new releases, sales, and giveaways.

WHERE TO FIND ME:
kaycorrell.com
authorcontact@kaycorrell.com

Join my Facebook Reader Group. We have lots
of fun and you'll hear about sales and new
releases first!
facebook.com/groups/KayCorrell/

I love to hear from my readers. Feel free to
contact me at authorcontact@kaycorrell.com

facebook.com/KayCorrellAuthor

instagram.com/kaycorrell

pinterest.com/kaycorrellauthor

amazon.com/author/kaycorrell

bookbub.com/authors/kay-correll